Notes from a
TOTALLY
LAME
VAMPIRE

Notes from a
TOTALLY
LAME
VAMPIRE
Because the Undead Have Feelings Too!

BY Tim Collins
ILLUSTRATED BY Andrew Pinder

ALADDIN • New York London Toronto Sydney

ALADDIN

An imprint of Simon & Schuster Children's Publishing Division

1230 Avenue of the Americas, New York, NY 10020

First Aladdin hardcover edition August 2010

Text and illustrations copyright © 2010 by Michael O'Mara Books Limited

Published by arrangement with Michael O'Mara Books Limited

Originally published in Great Britain in 2010 as Diary of a Wimpy Vampire by Michael O'Mara Books Limited

All rights reserved, including the right of reproduction in whole or in part in any form.

ALADDIN is a trademark of Simon & Schuster, Inc., and related logo is a registered trademark of Simon & Schuster, Inc.

For information about special discounts for bulk purchases, please contact Simon & Schuster Special Sales at 1-866-506-1949 or business@simonandschuster.com.

The Simon & Schuster Speakers Bureau can bring authors to your live event. For more information or to book an event contact the Simon & Schuster Speakers Bureau at 1-866-248-3049 or visit our website at www.simonspeakers.com.

Designed by Jessica Handelman

The text of this book was set in Carnes Handscript.

Manufactured in the United States of America 0710 FFG

10 9 8 7 6 5 4 3 2 1

Library of Congress Cataloging-in-Publication Data

Collins, Tim, 1975–

Notes from an utterly lame vampire : because the undead have feelings too! / written by Tim Collins; illustrations by Andrew Pinder. — 1st Aladdin ed.

p. cm.

Summary: High schooler Nigel, a 100-year-old vampire doomed to spend eternity in the body of a socially awkward fifteen-year-old boy, records his attempts to impress the love of his life, Chloe, while battling an embarrassingly overwhelming desire to sink his fangs into her.

ISBN 978-1-4424-1183-8 (pob ed.)

[1. Vampires—Fiction. 2. Love—Fiction. 3. Diaries—Fiction. 4. High schools—Fiction. 5. Schools—Fiction. 6. England—Fiction. 7. Humorous stories.] I. Pinder, Andrew, ill. II. Title.

PZ7.C69725No 2010

[Fic]—dc22

2010010634

# ACKNOWLEDGMENTS

Thanks to Lindsay Davies, Ana McLaughlin, Sarah Sandland, and everyone at Michael O'Mara Books. Thanks to Andrew Pinder for the illustrations. Finally, thanks as ever to Collette.

—T. C.

# SATURDAY, JANUARY 1

I shall turn one hundred this year, so I thought it was about time I kept a diary. Perhaps you're reading this in the future when some idiot has rammed a stake through my heart or chopped my head off. Perhaps you're a professor who's studying my poetry. Either way, welcome to my first ever diary!

Just because I said that I would turn one hundred this year, don't imagine me as an ancient old man. To your eyes, I would look like a kid, since that's what I was when the people I call my parents turned me into a vampire. They transformed me along with the girl I call my sister, as they felt like starting a family. And did they ask me about my feelings on the subject? Of course they didn't.

You might think that being undead is a nonstop thrill ride. Well, think again. Today was boring, and I've got another day to go until school starts again. I can't believe I'm looking forward to going back to that place. That should tell you how exciting things are round here!

## SUNDAY, JANUARY 2

It's quite hard to get the hang of writing diary entries. Humans probably start by saying what time they wake up, but I never sleep. I suppose I should start with what happened from midnight onward. Or maybe make 4:00 a.m. the cutoff point. It won't make much difference anyway, as all I ever do at night is play computer games.

If you're wondering why I don't run around all night drinking human blood, it's because Mum and Dad have to do all that stuff for me. When you transform into a vampire, your strength and speed are supposed to increase to superhuman levels. But what happened to me? Oh, that's right. Absolutely nothing. If anything, I got even weaker and slower than ever.

The annoying thing is, I still need blood to survive. But as it's too difficult for me to hunt, I have to rely on Mum and Dad to get it for me. Every few days they travel to a different town to get a fresh supply, because if they did it right here in Stockfield, everyone would realize we were vampires and put us in a zoo or something.

I hate being dependent on Mum and Dad, but I don't feel guilty about making them get the blood. After all, I didn't ask to be transformed. They got me into this mess, and fetching my meals every day is the very least they can do.

## MONDAY, JANUARY 3

A new girl has joined our school. She is called Chloe, and her family has just moved to town. She has pale skin, black eyes, and keeps her dark hair in a ponytail that shows off her long neck. She sat on her own in history, so I think she's scared of meeting new people. It will be interesting to see if she ends up making friends with the popular gang, the tough gang, or the Goths.

I'm sort of part of the Goths, but I don't hang around with them outside school or anything. I'm a bit of a mysterious loner, really.

Anyway, other than the new girl joining, it was a rather uneventful first day back. We had math with Mr. Wilson, and he said that we weren't concentrating enough because we were still too full of Christmas candy. He made the same joke last year, and I didn't laugh then, either. Nobody likes to ask him for help because he leans right over your shoulder and his breath smells of rancid coffee. People say the smell of garlic is lethal to vampires. Well, take it from me, it's got nothing on math-teacher coffee breath.

Had some type-A+ blood for dinner. It was quite bitter. You're supposed to say "Bless the sacred life force" before you drink it, but I'm too much of a rebel to bother with tradition.

I sat next to Chloe today in art, and I could smell that she had type-O blood, which is rare but especially tasty (my dad calls it the champagne of blood). I told her about the Goths, the tough gang, and the popular gang, and she said she wouldn't want to be in the popular gang. She is a girl after my own heart.

I told her about the rumor that Mr. Byrne was a millionaire before he lost all his money and had to become an English teacher, and about how Darren from our class came in on No Uniform Day wearing his PE stuff because those are the only clothes he owns. She didn't laugh at this and said she felt sorry for him, and I agreed, in order to make myself look caring and sensitive.

4:00 a.m.

I am in love with Chloe! I know this because I've been thinking about her since ten thirty. I can't stop picturing her dark eyes and her lovely pale neck.

I've had crushes on various girls before, but this is the real thing. Even if I could eat or sleep, I wouldn't be able to eat or sleep right now!

## WEDNESDAY, JANUARY 5

I sat next to Chloe in the library at lunchtime. Every time I stared at her, she looked down at her book instead of making eye contact. By rights, I should have mesmerized her with my intense, brooding beauty, but there was no sign of that.

Basically, I got the worst deal ever when I became a vampire. Every other vampire in history developed a supernatural level of attractiveness

8

when they transformed. But not me. When I look in the mirror*, I just see a pasty, tired, ninety-nine-year-old teenager looking back at me.

It's so unfair that I didn't get vampire beauty. I thought that was part of the deal. How am I supposed to attract humans to feed on? With my bubbly personality?

Anyway, I've resigned myself to the fact that I can't snare Chloe with my vampire

*Yes, vampires can see themselves in mirrors. Don't believe everything you see in horror films. Why would becoming a vampire mean that you couldn't see your reflection anymore? If they're going to make up lies about us, they could at least make sense.

good looks, so I'm going to have to do this the hard way, with charm.

## THURSDAY, JANUARY 6

A policeman showed us a road safety video in assembly this morning. It was really gory and upset some of the younger pupils, but it just made me feel thirsty. Sometimes I am ashamed of myself.

At lunchtime I went back to the library to sit next to Chloe. I wanted to talk to her, but I was too nervous. It was so humiliating. My kind has struck fear into the hearts of female humans for centuries. Why should I be the nervous one?

I can't even ask my parents for advice. They possess vampire beauty, so they wouldn't understand. I just wish they'd had the courtesy to pass it down to me.

Tonight I asked Dad what the best way to impress a girl is, and he said you should save her from death. But how am I supposed to do that without vampire strength? Buy her a bicycle helmet? Give her an antismoking leaflet? As ever, he's totally failed to appreciate what it's like for me.

## FRIDAY, JANUARY 7

An embarrassing thing happened today.

I was getting bored listening to Mr. Morris droning on about the Second World War, so I looked over at Chloe. As I focused on her I began to hear the sound of blood pumping around her veins, and I thought about what a wonderful relief it would be if I could pierce her jugular vein and have a refreshing sip. I got so hungry, I realized that my fangs had grown to twice their normal length!

To make the whole situation even more awkward, Mr. Morris then accused me of not paying attention and quizzed me about what he'd been saying. I know all about the Second World War, because I remember it very well, but I couldn't say anything in case anyone saw my fangs, so he went nuts at me.

# SATURDAY, JANUARY 8

After all the stress of last week I wanted nothing more than to lie around the house today and think about Chloe. No chance of that, though. Dad barged in at six this morning and announced that we were going for a hike.*

I hate family hike days. As I lack vampire strength and speed, I'm always trundling along behind the rest of them as they bound back and forth like undead Labradors.

Even my little sister runs ahead of me on family hikes. She has vampire strength and speed, but good luck getting her to admit this when Mum and Dad want her to do something around the house.

---

*Technically, they're my "coven" rather than my family, and we live in a "lair" rather than a house. I don't see the point in these formal terms, though.

Today's hike was around the wild countryside north of Stockfield, and the three of them kept zipping around and telling me about the lakes, hills, and forests I was missing out on. Like I even cared.

We came across a wide river, and they crossed it by leaping hundreds of feet up in the air. Dad offered to carry me across on his back, but I told them I'd wait in the car.

And it's in my dad's Volvo that I now reside, Dear Diary, thinking about my sweet, sweet Chloe. I have been sitting here for three hours now, gazing at the tempestuous, turbulent clouds racing across the windswept landscape . . . so this is what being in love is like!

## SUNDAY, JANUARY 9

Annoying things about my sister Part One Million:

She's decided that she wants to drink animal blood rather than human blood from now on. She says she's doing this for "ethical reasons." One of her friends must have taught her that phrase because she's used it about fifty times today.

What ethical reasons? Feeding on humans doesn't kill them, unless the vampire in question is so greedy that they drain every last drop of their blood. It won't even turn them into vampires if you don't mix blood with them.

All that happens to humans is they're mes-merized, drained of a couple of pints of blood, left feeling a bit woozy, and have to take a couple of days off work. When you think about it, vampires are no more evil than a case of flu.

Anyway, my sister says she only wants to drink animal blood now, so today they've all driven off to gather it from cows and sheep. Needless to say, I'm refusing to take any part in this charade. My sister is only going to make herself ill by refusing to drink human blood. As long as she doesn't come crying to me when she's weak with hunger, it's of no interest to me.

NOTE: If you are actually my sister and you're reading this, I don't care if I've upset you. It's no less than you deserve for reading the secret words of others.

UPDATE: I have decided that every night I will tape a hair over the end of my diary. If the hair is broken, I will know my sister has been looking in here.

MONDAY, JANUARY 10
12:20 p.m.

I am sitting opposite Chloe in the library writing this. She's always here at lunchtime. This either means she doesn't have any friends yet or she's a brain. I hope she's a brain, because that way none of the other boys will like her and I'll have a better chance. Perhaps in a minute she'll look over and ask me what I'm writing.

12:55 p.m.

Lunch is coming to an end now and Chloe has not yet asked me what I'm writing. I think I need to be more proactive. I shall find out more about her interests. She is currently looking at a book about animals, so I shall pretend I'm interested in them, even though the truth of the matter is that I hate them because they freak out if I go anywhere near them.

## 2:00 a.m.
Mum and Dad were playing funeral marches at full volume tonight, which made it really hard for me to concentrate on learning animal facts. When they finally went upstairs, they left all the candles on. I must have told them a thousand times that this could cause a fire.

## TUESDAY, JANUARY 11
I think I'm bonding with Chloe. Perhaps she'll yield to my immortal allure soon.

I reeled off my animal facts in the library this
lunchtime. She seemed quite impressed, and we
had a good chat.

Later on she offered me a piece of candy. It

was supposed to be lime flavored, but like anything that isn't blood, it tasted of coal dipped
in vomit to me. When she wasn't looking, I spat
the rotten thing into the trash. But I kept the
wrapper as a relic of my love.

I shall tell her about this when we're married
and we shall laugh.

To get rid of the taste, I went to the rest-
room for lunch. I understand that this might sound
rather unpleasant, but this is the only way I can
feed at school. Every day I take a thermos of
blood to school as a packed lunch. Since I can't
sit in the cafeteria with blood dribbling down my
chin, I have to lock myself in a bathroom stall to
enjoy it. I understand that as dining experiences
go, this is unlikely to get a Michelin star, but it's
the only safe place for me to drink. I once tried
it crouching down behind the garbage cans, but

someone saw me with blood all around my mouth and I had to pretend I'd fallen over.

### WEDNESDAY, JANUARY 12
#### 6:00 p.m.

I couldn't find Chloe at lunchtime, so I went to the bleachers behind the gym and hung around with the Goths instead.

The Goths are called Brian, John, and Si, and if you call them the Goths, they say they're really emos. I think Brian only joined the group because he's fat and it doesn't show as much when you wear black. I think Si joined because he's got red hair that he hates and now he can dye his hair black. It's hard to tell why John joined because he never says anything. As for me, I don't really hang round with them out of choice. It's just that my pale skin and black clothing sort of automatically place me in their gang.

Brian has a girlfriend who goes to another school. I thought he might be lying until he showed me a picture of her. Nobody would pretend to have a girlfriend who looked like that.

4:00 a.m.
I can't stop thinking about Chloe. Is it normal

for a vampire to be this attracted to a human? I wish there were someone I could talk to.

## THURSDAY, JANUARY 13

Our science lesson today was about the heart, and the teacher kept going on about how the heart pumps blood around the atria and ventricles. Needless to say, I got so thirsty that my fangs extended for the entire lesson and I had to bury my head in my textbook.

At the end of the lesson, we were given color handouts with explicit pictures of hearts, veins, and blood cells. I took mine home and hid it underneath my mattress.

I sat with Chloe again at lunchtime, and she told me she's agreed to be a class officer. Her duties will include reporting people who run in the corridors or cause disruption in assembly. I don't think this will win her a lot of popularity, but I respect her maturity and fully intend to defend her against those who tease her for it. As long as I don't have to fight anyone.

## FRIDAY, JANUARY 14

Chloe fell over and cut her knee on the way to the library today, and a small trickle of delicious type O ran down her leg. I got so hungry that I had to go off and gulp down the contents of my thermos.

As I ran away I could see that Wayne from my class came to Chloe's aid. What must she think of me for running away like that? Why am I so cursed? How can I explain myself? Maybe I can pretend that I have a phobia about blood rather than a thirst for it. Either way, she's going to think I'm a weirdo.

# SATURDAY, JANUARY 15

Today I offered to help Mum and Dad clean the house. We only moved here six months ago, and it already looks like a ruined Gothic castle. I know they feel more comfortable surrounded by thick velvet curtains, golden candelabras, and ancient oil paintings, but the place is too gloomy and dusty. I bet child protective services wouldn't be too impressed if they paid a visit.

My parents rejected my offer, saying that

I'd only throw something expensive away by mistake. So what should I do, then? Wait for them to clean up? Let's just say it's a good thing we've got the rest of eternity for that!

This afternoon my sister asked me if I wanted to play soccer with her in the back garden. I said no, just like I did the last thousand times she asked. I don't know why she thinks I'm suddenly going to change my mind.

All that happens is that we take turns shooting penalties while the other goes in goal. It's all very one-sided, thanks to my sister's speed and strength. I'll take five penalties, which she'll save in the unlikely event that they go near the goal, and then she'll take five penalties. Even if I do catch the ball, the force of it whacks me into the back of the net, and she counts it as a goal. We broke the greenhouse at our last house when the force of one of her penalties knocked me through it.

So, even if I was remotely interested in soccer, getting beaten at it by a ten-year-old girl would hardly be my idea of fun.

## SUNDAY, JANUARY 16

My stupid sister is upset because she wants to change her name and Mum and Dad won't let her. Her name is Mavis (and has been since she was born in 1916), but now she's being teased in school for having an old-fashioned name and wants to change it to something modern.

Quite sensibly, Mum and Dad have told her that she has to wait until next time we move rather than suddenly announcing to her class that she's changed her name. However, they might have been more likely to give in if her ideas

hadn't been so ridiculous. Her list of suggested
names in order of preference was:

Twist
Princess
Jet
Sailor
Melody
Orchid
Manhattan
Angel

Like she wouldn't draw attention to herself
with any of those!
Anyway, Mum and Dad put their foot down with
her for the first time in a century, and now she's
stormed off to her room. I am resisting chanting

the name "Mavis" outside her door, because I'm too mature to care. I might just go and shout it a couple of times, though.

## MONDAY, JANUARY 17

I sat next to Chloe in the library at lunchtime so I could apologize for dashing off on Friday, but she didn't say anything about it, so I let it go.

I wanted to talk to her, but whenever I tried, I kept getting thirsty and could feel my fangs growing again. It's not like I only want to sink my teeth into her neck. I want to get to know her and have meaningful conversations with her and take her for long moonlit walks. Obviously, it would be nice if she let me drink her blood, too, but that's not all I'm interested in.

I'm so confused by my feelings.

# TUESDAY, JANUARY 18

12:05 p.m.

I'm in the library sitting next to Chloe again.
Perhaps I'm putting her off by smiling too much.
I once read that humans are attracted to the
smoldering intensity of vampires. I will now make
an effort to pout.

12:10 p.m.

It's actually quite difficult to pout. I probably
should have practiced in front of the mirror.

Look up from your textbook, Chloe, and see the doomed longing of the decades etched upon my melancholy features! Look up from your textbook and yield to icy bliss! Look up from your textbook because my face is starting to hurt now!

12:15 p.m.
Chloe looked up from her textbook and asked if I was feeling ill. Pouting attempt deemed a failure.

## WEDNESDAY, JANUARY 19

Mum dropped me off at school today, and it was a very embarrassing experience. Like all vampires except me, she appears overwhelmingly beautiful to humans. This is all well and good when she's catching prey, but not great for me if I want to get through the school day without being teased.

I told her to stay in the car, but she insisted on kissing me on the cheek in front of everyone.

By lunchtime the whole pathetic school was buzzing with the news that I had a "hot mum" and I couldn't walk down the corridors without some idiot asking if they could go on a date with her.

It would serve them right if I did set them up with her. They'd end up lying in an alley drained of blood after five minutes.

Why can't I just have normal parents like everyone else?

## THURSDAY, JANUARY 20

Today was cold but bright, and I got a couple of unpleasant zits on my chin. It's sometimes said that sunlight kills vampires, but this is another myth. Bright sunlight makes a vampire's skin burn, but it's only a mild irritant, not much worse than what someone with red hair would experience. This is the real reason we avoid hot countries and prefer to go out at night, and the origin of all those silly ideas about us turning to ash if we forget the clocks have changed and open the curtains at the wrong time.

As usual, I got a particularly bad deal, as the sun gives me terrible acne as well as a rash. In the summer I cover my face in high-SPF sunblock every few hours, and that gives me decent protection. But there are days like today when rays unexpectedly hit my face and I get a nasty cluster of whiteheads. It's annoying, but it beats turning into the contents of an overturned ashtray, I suppose.

I was too ashamed to sit next to Chloe at lunchtime with my hideous zits. I shall cover them up with white foundation tomorrow.

## FRIDAY, JANUARY 21

Mum and Dad have gone down to London today to do boring bank stuff. Sometimes I go down with them, but I couldn't today because I had school.

Although London is an exciting city, it makes me feel sad when I see how much it's changed since we lived there in the thirties. The neon signs at Piccadilly Circus have changed from Wrigley's gum and Schweppes to McDonald's. And in all that time I still haven't got a girl-friend. I need to sort my life out.

My parents don't need jobs because we live off the interest of the many bank accounts they've opened over the years. However, we're not allowed to spend too much in case it draws attention to us. I only get ten pounds a week allowance, which is totally unfair when you con-sider I'm the son of millionaires.

1:00 a.m.

My sister is so annoying! She's got her music on

at full blast, and she won't turn it down! Mum and Dad are still out, and she won't obey me.

For a vampire, her taste in music is an absolute disgrace. She's listening to some dreadful pop song about how true beauty is on the inside, written by cynical old songwriters for a manufactured teen starlet. Vampires are supposed to like funeral marches, dirges, and haunting piano pieces. If we must listen to modern music,

we should at the very least listen to emo, Goth, or death metal. Teen pop is surely inappropriate for the undead.

Plus, if these songwriters really believe that true beauty comes from within and not from physical appearances, why didn't they get someone unattractive, like Brian's girlfriend, to sing it rather than a sixteen-year-old starlet who looks like she's been created from scratch by a plastic surgeon?

## SATURDAY, JANUARY 22

Mum and Dad are back from London, but they are both unwell. I don't know what kind of blood they drank down there, but they look pale, even by vampire standards. I suspect they fed on someone with a high level of alcohol in their blood, which we're supposed to avoid. In

theory, the smell of alcohol should have been enough to repel them, but I bet they went right ahead and glugged away, anyway, the greedy pigs.

And what happens to me in these situations? Oh, that's right, I miss out on meals altogether. They know I'm not strong enough to hunt humans myself, and yet they merrily stuff their faces with questionable blood, not caring about the consequences. I wish they'd think about someone else for once in their lives.

## SUNDAY, JANUARY 23

Mum and Dad are still ill, and now I'm feeling weak due to lack of blood. I can't skip school next week, as I shall miss the chance to see Chloe, and someone will steal her from me.

Wait, my true love! I shall find my strength!

## MONDAY, JANUARY 24

I went in to school today, although I'm still weak from lack of blood. If any of the teachers were observant enough to notice my condition, I'd get taken into foster care.

Chloe smiled at me in math today, but I was

so hungry that my fangs came out and I couldn't smile back. If only I could express my true feelings for her. I might write a poem.

## 2:00 a.m.

Dad has finally seen fit to go out and get us some more blood. He even had the nerve to tell me off for not thanking him when he brought it to me. I would have thanked him if I'd had the strength, the selfish old corpse!

## 4:00 a.m.

I have written my poem now, and I think it shows how deep my feelings are. It's a symbolic poem, as it uses actual light and dark to stand for the lightness and darkness of my moods. I considered mailing it to Chloe, but I've decided to wait before sharing it.

# I WALK IN SHADOW

I walk in shadow

Shielding my dark desire

You walk in sunlight

Your eyes afire

To join you in the light

Oh, how I long

But it gives me zits

And my skin feels all wrong


## TUESDAY, JANUARY 25

Mrs. Maguire did an assembly about religious tolerance today, and I went home sick.

She started her talk by showing us a crucifix on the overhead projector, which wasn't great for me. Although it's not true that crucifixes make vampires recoil in terror, they can give us headaches. And it's not just crucifixes, either.

41

I can get a stinking migraine from any religious symbol. Which is why I began to feel queasy when Mrs. Maguire proceeded to show us the symbols of every other major religion. I got as far as the star and crescent and the yin and yang before I had to make a dash for the exit, reeling like I was on a ferry in a storm.

I've been lying down for a while and feel better now. At least I've got PE to look forward to tomorrow. Not.

## WEDNESDAY, JANUARY 26

PE was even worse than expected. I didn't want anyone to notice my pale skin while I was getting changed, so I tried to get into my PE uniform really quickly and ended up tripping onto the floor.

We then had to go to the gym and jump over

a vaulting horse. I couldn't manage it, so Mr. Jenkins said I had to do push-ups on the crash mat as punishment. I really hate Mr. Jenkins. I hate him more than any other PE teacher I have ever had, which is saying a lot, as I must have had about forty over the years and they tend to represent the absolute lowest form of humanity.

Luckily for me, Chloe is in a different PE class. If she'd seen my humiliation at the hands of the evil Mr. Jenkins, there's no way she'd ever like me.

# THURSDAY, JANUARY 27

11:00 a.m.

We got our science homework back today and I got a C. It's not a very good grade, but it's not bad enough to get me moved down in the class.

You'd think that after studying a subject for over eighty years, I'd be better at it. But the weird thing is that I can't apply myself because I know that soon we'll move towns and I'll start the school year all over again and get another chance to learn it. As long as I do enough to coast along, my parents don't tell me off. I'm pretty good at history, especially the bits that happened in my lifetime. I'm also really good at playing the piano, which I learned before we had a TV, but Dad won't let me study music at school in case it draws attention to us. Anyone would think he would be proud of his son's talent.

# FRIDAY, JANUARY 28

Mrs. Maguire told me off after assembly today for refusing to sing along with the hymns. I wasn't doing it to break the rules; I was just worried that I would get a bad headache again, like when I looked at the crucifix. At any rate, it's better not to sing at all than to sing obscene alternative words like Wayne and Craig did.

In the library at lunchtime, Chloe said she admired me for sticking to my principles as an atheist, so at least some good came out of it. She gave me a piece of gum, and her hand touched mine for a brief, forbidden moment. Like all vampires, my body temperature is very low, and Chloe seemed surprised by how cold my hand was. It's easier to get away with this in January than it will be in summer, but by then she'll know of my true nature.

I need to make a move on Chloe. When I'm back in school on Monday, I'll invite her out on a date. Or I might wait until Tuesday.

## SATURDAY, JANUARY 29

Today we had our annual family trip to Whitby. It's really boring, and I've been there loads of times before. It's the place where Mum and Dad first lived when they came over from France, so they go back there to talk about boring nostalgic things every year. It's also the place where Dracula first arrives in England in Bram Stoker's novel, which has led Dad to speculate that the character was based on him. Personally, I think it's just a coincidence. Dracula does lots of silly things in that book, like transforming into a bat, a dog, and even some fog, so it's clearly a work of wild imagination written by someone who's never even met a vampire.

On the way back from Whitby, Mum and Dad tried to strike up a conversation, but I

didn't feel like talking. I heard them mutter-
ing something about how I'm just going through
a phase. I was going to explain to them that
when something goes on for eighty-five years,
it hardly counts as a phase, but I couldn't be
bothered. They wouldn't understand.

Mum and Dad wanted to play Scrabble when
we got back, but I wasn't interested. They
always cheat by making up words like "zaqox"
and pretending they were really popular in the
nineteenth century.

## SUNDAY, JANUARY 30

Today I looked on the Internet for tips about
asking girls out, but when Dad saw that I was
on the computer, he got really annoyed.

He thinks that all computers are dangerous,
even though he doesn't understand them at all.

He barely got the hang of typewriters before they went out of fashion.

Dad's convinced that someone or other is going to trace us all through the Internet. What does he think I'm doing, tagging a photo of him drinking blood on Facebook? And who is he so worried about, anyway? He's always told me that we are the last four vampires left on earth, so it can't be any of our own kind that he fears. And as for human enemies, anyone he's offended in the past must surely be too old to be a threat by now.

I tried to show Dad the fun side of the Internet by showing him a clip of a panda sneezing, but I don't think he understood it was supposed to be funny. If anything, I think it just made him hungry.

Dad's so out of date he makes me cringe.

Once, when Mum was planning a surprise party for my sister, he suggested that we get some hunchbacks with bells on to dance for her. I can't believe he thought that would be appropriate. That's not been considered an acceptable form of entertainment for centuries now.

## MONDAY, JANUARY 31
12:00 p.m.

I've decided to ask my parents to buy me a car to compensate for the extra speed I should have gotten when I became a vampire. It's the least they can do, really. I know they can afford it, so they have no reason to refuse me other than spite. Based on observations I've made of older boys, I've decided that Chloe would be more likely to go out with me if I had a car.

My parents won't buy me a car, as they say I don't look old enough to drive it and it will draw too much attention to us. I even offered to wear a false beard every time I drive, but they still refused.

I told them that I don't care what they think because they're not my real parents, anyway, and then ran up to my room and slammed the door.

It's so unfair. My sister gets absolutely everything she wants, but they refuse all of my simple requests.

12:00 a.m.

I spent tonight feeling really angry with my parents for refusing to buy me a car, but I've calmed down now. I know I get annoyed with them, but I should at least be grateful that I'm not one of those vampire kids with vampire parents who appear to be older but are younger than them.* Then it would be really annoying if they were strict with you.

---

*This might sound impossible, but it's quite simple, really. Imagine if my dad had been born as a human a few years later than me, but not transformed into a vampire until he was in his thirties or forties. To the eyes of a human he would look older than me, but I would know he was younger. And ignore everything he said.

I looked in the bathroom mirror this morning and noticed that my zits have gotten worse. Sometimes I wish vampires really couldn't see their reflections.

1:00 p.m.

Chloe was upset today when the girls from the popular gang wouldn't let her sit at their table because she reported them for talking in assembly. I agreed that they were being completely unfair, as she was only doing her duty as an officer.

We then had a good chat about a ghost-hunting show that was on TV last night. They had some actors from a soap opera staying in an old country house, and it filmed them listening to strange noises. Chloe thought it was fake, and I agreed with her.

I can remember getting scared of ghosts when I was at school in the fifties. We used to think that one of the corridors was haunted by a student who drowned, and we would always run down it so he couldn't get us. Looking back, it was a bit hypocritical of me to be so scared of a supernatural entity despite being one myself, but I was much more easily swayed back then.

5:00 p.m.
It's PE again tomorrow. I can't face another lesson with that idiot Mr. Jenkins, so I'm going to ask Dad for a note to get me out of it. I'll get him to write that I've got a bad back and that I can't do PE for three months.

# WEDNESDAY, FEBRUARY 2

At first Dad refused to give me a note to get out of PE. He said it was the best lesson in school and I should be looking forward to it. That's easy for him to say, with his vampire strength and speed. PE might well be fun if you can run a marathon in five minutes and leap over hurdles as if they were paper clips. I can't even do a somersault!

In the end he agreed to write the note but still managed to make it embarrassing. He went off into his study and wrote on ancient parchment with a quill. That might have been acceptable in the seventeenth century, but it isn't now. I wish he would make at least some effort to get with the times.

Mr. Jenkins almost had a heart attack when I gave him the note, but he accepted it nonetheless, and I enjoyed a blissful PE-free afternoon in the library.

## THURSDAY, FEBRUARY 3

We had a science test this morning that I'd completely forgotten about. I hadn't done any studying, and I got it all wrong. It's so horrible when you scan through the questions on a test and realize you can't do any of them. I don't know why humans think vampires are scary. Tests are much worse.

This afternoon I found out that the girls from the popular gang have given every boy in the class a mark out of ten for looks. I don't care what the popular gang thinks about me, but I hope I didn't get less than seven. I'm supposed to be a beautiful, aristocratic immortal. I'd be the first to admit that I'm not the best-looking vampire of all time, but I'd still like to think that I'm better than average-looking.

Jay from the tough gang waited outside the school gates tonight and gave everyone a deadarm on the way home (this is when he hits you so hard at the top of your arm that it goes numb). I didn't mind because I can't feel pain. Technically, the whole of me is dead, so a deadarm isn't a big deal.

# FRIDAY, FEBRUARY 4

Craig has seen the list of marks out of ten, and apparently I got a four! According to him, only three people in the class got a worse score than me! And they include Darren, who has fleas.

Why do none of the girls fancy me? I'm a vampire—I should be the class heartthrob. Judging from my score, I'm more Quasimodo than Count Dracula.

I have thick black hair and deep-set eyes, although I'm not good at eye contact. My skin is pure white when it's not plagued with rashes or acne. I'm also quite tall for my age, and I would surely have grown to over six feet if I'd stayed human longer.

Why don't these elements combine to produce the deadly, hypnotic beauty that's rightfully mine?

Perhaps one day they will, and all the girls in the popular gang will be begging to go out with me. And I will laugh in their silly little faces.

## SATURDAY, FEBRUARY 5

I asked Dad today about why I don't have the same attractiveness as other vampires, and he suggested it was to do with the age I trans-formed. He said that supernatural beauty is something grown-up vampires need to attract prey, but vampire children don't need it because they have their parents to get food for them.

Could he be any more patronizing? For a start, I wasn't a child when I transformed, and I was mature for my age, so you'd think that the laws of vampire biology would have made an exception.

He also said that you don't hear my sister complaining about it. Of course she doesn't. She hates boys and would be happy enough to spend the rest of eternity getting pampered by my indulgent parents. All I can say is that she'd better hope they don't bump into any vampire slayers, as I have no intention of looking after her if they aren't around.

He did make one useful suggestion, though. He said that to humans, vampires smell of the thing they most desire. He suggested that I might be stifling my natural vampire aroma with deodorant. I know he dislikes the smell of the stuff I spray on every morning, so he might just be saying this to make me stop using it, but I'll try cutting it out next week and see if it makes me more alluring.

## SUNDAY, FEBRUARY 6

Today we had a family trip to the seaside. My sister insisted that we all go on the ghost-train ride at the amusement park even though it always makes her frightened. She had to bury her head in Mum's gown when the carriage went past a luminous skeleton (or "skellington," as she pronounces it). It was so pathetic.

The man in the ticket booth was dressed as a vampire, though he wasn't putting much effort in. In fact, he was the first vampire I've ever seen who looked even more bored than me! He was also seriously overweight, which wouldn't be possible for a real vampire. We live off human blood, not deep-crust pizzas.

## MONDAY, FEBRUARY 7

As suspected, Dad was talking nonsense about the whole vampire-smell thing. I've been off the deodorant since Saturday, but far from attracting anyone, I ended up sitting on my own in every lesson today.

In math, I even stretched out my arms to see if the smell of my untreated pits would get the humans flocking around. Instead, everyone in the row behind me pulled their sweaters up over their noses to protect themselves from the stink.

I concluded that my natural smell is probably not attractive to humans, so I avoided Chloe for the rest of the day. I clearly don't smell of the thing humans most desire.

Unless the thing humans most desire is a cheese sand-wich that's been accidentally left in a locker over the summer vacation.

## TUESDAY, FEBRUARY 8

Today I heard a piece of news that pierced my heart like a stake dipped in garlic and holy water. Wayne likes Chloe!

I must act soon! I'll never forgive myself if she starts going out with that fool. I'm sure she won't be interested in him, though. He hangs around with the popular gang, and he's quite good at soccer, I'll admit. But he's got bad teeth and a downy mustache and he's in the bottom class for English, where they let you watch DVDs instead of reading books. My wonderful Chloe couldn't possibly fall for anyone that stupid.

If only I could tell you the truth, Chloe! When

he's middle-aged and bald, I'll be here for you, just as young and attractive as ever. Or, at least, just as young as ever.

Tomorrow, my beautiful prey, I shall reveal all.

## WEDNESDAY, FEBRUARY 9
### 10:00 p.m.

I went to the library to reveal the truth about my nature to Chloe, but I was too nervous to say anything, so I went to the steps at the back of the library to hang around with my annoying friends, the school Goths, instead.

They were talking about a new vampire show that started on TV last night, and weren't they just the world's leading authorities on the subject? Si got the ball of ignorance rolling by trotting out the myth that vampires can transform themselves into bats. Oh, can they, now? And what happens to our bones when we do this? Do they magically shrink and then expand again? And what about our clothes? Do they somehow appear again when we transform back to human form, or are we naked? It would hardly be worth using your bat power if it meant having to spend the rest of the day with no clothes on.

Next, Brian said that he wished he were a vampire. I was so incensed by this that I was tempted to sink my fangs into his ample neck right then and show him the dull reality behind his childish fantasy. He'd be bored out of his mind in minutes, with no extra-large pizza or afternoon nap to look forward to.

Then, worst of all, John said that he preferred zombies, anyway. Zombies? What have those stinking corpses got to do with vampires?

How is this a legitimate comparison? And even if zombies did exist, what kind of cretin would prefer them to pale, beautiful immortals?

I utterly despair of these idiots I am forced to call my friends.

3:00 a.m.

I've been having a think about what it would be like if I really could transform into a bat and fly to Chloe's house. Sometimes I wish the myths about vampires were true!

# THURSDAY, FEBRUARY 10

## 10:00 a.m.

The girls from my class all fancy the actor from the vampire TV show, and they've covered their notebooks with pictures of him in serious and moody poses. How blind of them to obsess over this manufactured image of vampirism when they have the real thing right under their noses.

Sometimes I think these shallow humans don't deserve my company.

## 6:00 p.m.

In art today I drew a charcoal picture of a girl fleeing in terror from a vampire in a graveyard. The girl was wearing a white dress and looked like Chloe, while the vampire was wearing a cape and looked like me. It was a very corny and inaccurate depiction, but I must admit I found it rather thrilling.

I got worried that Chloe would notice the drawing, so I went over it until it turned into abstract shapes. My artistic talent, like my musical talent and my literary talent, must remain cloaked for now.

The art teacher asked me what the abstract shapes represented, and I said "Desire." I think she was quite impressed.

FRIDAY, FEBRUARY 11
2:00 p.m.

We did cooking in home economics today, which is always boring for me because I don't eat. I only took the subject as my elective because the alternative was design and technology, and I've heard that includes smoothing down wooden poles

69

on the lathe. Imagine if I tripped and staked myself on one of those things! I'm surprised they even allow it.

We were supposed to be making spaghetti bolognaise, and Mrs. Molloy told me off for not draining the water before I added the tinned tomatoes. Why would I care? It's going straight in the garbage, anyway.

Later I told Chloe how much I hate cooking, and she said she hates it too! We have so much in common, we must be soul mates.

Chloe said that she doesn't care about cooking because she doesn't want to end up as a housewife. She wouldn't have to do any cooking if she were my wife. Or any housework at all if she didn't want to. All she would have to do is stand on a moonlit balcony and offer her perfect white neck to me.

The principal has announced that there will be a special Valentine's mail service on Monday. I have just seventy-two hours to compose a message to write in my card to Chloe. Let's just say that my math textbook will be ignored this weekend!

## SATURDAY, FEBRUARY 12

This morning I went to the newsstand near the station and bought the biggest card they had. It's over fifty centimeters high and features a love heart and a border of red roses. I'm not sure why humans think that particular shape resembles the heart, as it doesn't look like one to me. Personally, I'd prefer the image of an actual pumping heart, like you'd see in biology textbooks.

Anyway, I'm guessing that the card is the kind of thing that female humans find appealing. Now to compose an appropriate message . . .

Have a nice Valentine's Day. (Too weak.)

Sending you sincere wishes on this Valentine's Day. (Too formal.)

I've been watching you, but you don't know. (Too creepy.)

Roses are red, violets are blue, I've waited a century for a girl like you. (Too corny.)

I've searched through the frozen mists of eternity for you. (Too vampirey.)

Yield to the forbidden music of my soul. (Way too vampirey.)

Dear Chloe, please can I sink my teeth into your neck and drink your blood? (One step at a time, Nigel.)

## SUNDAY, FEBRUARY 13

I have chosen the message for my card. . . .

In eternal admiration, love from ?

As you can see, it has a clever double meaning, because my admiration really is eternal, as I'm immortal.* I have practiced writing the message ten times in fancy handwriting, and now I shall put it in the card.

## MONDAY, FEBRUARY 14

A worrying development today.

Although my card was the biggest, Chloe got a total of three Valentine's cards! Three! I know she's beautiful, but I presumed nobody else would like her because she's a brain.

How am I going to fend off two love rivals?

I was so worried, I hardly noticed that I didn't get a single card myself. But just imagine the

---

*Some pedants complain when this word is used to describe vampires, as we can be killed if you ram a stake through our hearts or lop our heads off. But I'm happy to use it because it sounds cool. Anyway, I'd like to see those pedants heal broken bones in a matter of minutes.

scene if I possessed the vampiric good looks that should be mine. A desk piled high with cards, every pair of female eyes in the room fixed on me, my dark hunter's eyes meeting Chloe's expectant gaze, and my voice burning with ancient wisdom as I proclaim my love for her.

Instead, I get one less card than flea-ridden Darren. I am truly a creature of the damned.

# TUESDAY, FEBRUARY 15

Though it annoyed me to do so, I sat at a table with the girls from the popular gang to catch up on the Valentine's gossip. Based on their information, I've compiled a table of suspected love rivals:

| NAME | LIKELIHOOD | THREAT LEVEL |
|------|-----------|--------------|
| Wayne Cross  | Very high—told Peter Ellen he liked her, and Peter told Samantha Jackson. | Low—he has bad teeth and even more zits than me, and is from a rougher area of town than Chloe, so there would be a class barrier like in *Wuthering Heights* (which we're doing in English). |
| Gary Martin  | High—walked her home once. | Low—he has rich parents but attends lunchtime chess club and smells of disinfectant. |

| Craig Hooper | High—posted eight cards in total. | Medium—he is the best-looking boy in our year, but he says he's a ladies' man and doesn't want to commit himself to one woman. |
| --- | --- | --- |

| Sanjay Bhatti | Unknown. | High—his parents live on the same street as hers, so he would have ample opportunity. |
| --- | --- | --- |

| Darren Riley | Unlikely—cannot afford card. | Moderate—although girls don't usually like him, Chloe is very caring and feels pity for social outcasts. |
| --- | --- | --- |

| John the Goth | Unknown—too quiet. | Low—too quiet. |
| --- | --- | --- |

I feel slightly better about the situation now that I've completed my table. Although there are some potential threats out there, I am convinced Chloe will be mine if I act fast.

# WEDNESDAY, FEBRUARY 16

Jay from the tough gang charged me fifty pence just to walk past him in the corridor this afternoon. It was so humiliating. I should be striking fear into the hearts of mortals, not unwillingly contributing to their next pair of sneakers.

I attempted to talk to Chloe about Valentine's cards in the library at lunchtime to see if she'd worked out that I sent the best one. I tried to steer the conversation round to the topic by asking her if she'd had a good week and if anything unusual had happened. She wasn't taking the bait, so in the end I had to come right out and ask her if she got any cards. She said no and then looked down at her book, blushing a deep red. Her delectable blood filled her cheeks and in my head it sounded like stormy waves crashing on a beach. We stayed in this awkward stalemate for the rest of lunch, with her staring down at her textbook and me drawing on every ounce of self-restraint to prevent myself from telling her the truth right there in front of everyone.

It was actually quite a relief when she had to go to business studies.

## THURSDAY, FEBRUARY 17

There's been a vampire attack right here in town! I'm so angry with Mum and Dad, the greedy pigs! Why can't they hold back from their blood-drinking urges?

The worst thing is, they wouldn't even own up to it. I only found out because Mr. Talbot, the school caretaker, was looking a bit pale and I asked him about his health. He said he'd collapsed on the weekend and blacked out for a couple of hours. He had to stay in bed for a couple of days, but just as he was about to see a doctor, he started to feel better. He kept scratching his neck, and when I looked closely, I saw a couple of telltale fang marks on it.

I confronted Mum and Dad about their

behavior as soon as I got home, but they insisted that they'd only been feeding in towns over twenty miles away, which was our agreement. I don't know why they insist on lying to me. It's obvious that they were too thirsty to wait until they were farther away and fed off poor old Mr. Talbot instead. So, just because they couldn't contain their urges, they risked exposing our identity and forcing us to flee this town, meaning that I would never see my dear Chloe again. In other words, they put their own stupid thirst above my first ever chance of happiness! How can I trust them again?

FRIDAY, FEBRUARY 18
8:30 a.m.

We don't have to go to school today because it's snowing. My sister ran into my room at six

to announce this like it was the most exciting thing that had ever happened. She must
have opened her curtains to see snow a million
times by now, but it still makes her giddy with
excitement.

She's so stupid that I wonder if she even
knows she's been alive for almost a century.
Perhaps she has no sense of time passing at
all, like a goldfish swimming around a bowl.

When you're as dense as my sister, living forever is a breeze. But when you're
as sensitive and intelligent as me, it's not
easy. Not that I expect anyone to understand.

From the excited laughter I can hear outside my window, I'm guessing that everyone
else shares my sister's idiotic joy that a snow
day happened just before break. All it means

to me is that I have to wait ten long days before I see my darling Chloe again.

10:00 a.m.

My sister has built a snowpire using carrots for fangs and a trash bag for a cape. I thought my parents would tell her off for exposing our identity, but they seemed to think it was the most ador-able thing they'd ever seen. As ever, it's one rule for me and one rule for my sister.

Dad said it was the only vampire he'd ever seen that really would be destroyed by sunlight, and then he laughed at his own stupid joke.

1:00 p.m.

I am so bored, I am now watching Sesame Street. I have to say, I find the character of the Count somewhat offensive. He has a huge nose, pointy ears, and a ridiculous Eastern European accent. They wouldn't get away with doing this about any other minority group.

If they insist on showing all the usual clichéd stuff like castles and bats, they could at least balance it out by showing the positive side of vampirism as well, like our unnatural beauty and strength.

Plus, if they're going to show a vampire with a rank of nobility, why does it always have to be a count? They would find that vampires have also been archdukes, barons, knights, margraves, viscounts, and kings if they spent more time researching and less time making up silly jokes about us counting things.

SATURDAY, FEBRUARY 19

7:00 a.m.

Mum and Dad are out hunting, and I'm expecting a bumper harvest of blood. They always get loads when it's snowing, as it makes humans much easier to trap and mesmerize.

I can't wait to see what kind they bring back. If you're a human and you're reading this, you might think it must be boring for me to drink blood all the time. But I think it must be boring to eat food all the time.

There are so many different flavors and textures of blood that it never feels like you're having the same thing over and over again. Sometimes, if it's a special occasion, we even have a three-course meal, starting with a glass of something light and thin like type A-, tucking into hot bowls of thick, nourishing type B+, and finishing with a sweet dessert blood from someone with high blood-sugar levels.

5:00 p.m.

Good news! Mum and Dad have brought back loads of lovely type O-. And the best thing is, they've harvested so many bottles of it they couldn't even fit them in the fridge, and they've let me take some up to my room for a feast!

7:00 p.m.

Having a good time getting through the blood. Starting to feel a bit stuffed, but it would be a shame to waste all this lovely stuff. I imagine this is what humans feel like on Christmas Day.

9:00 p.m.

Still getting through the bottles. Have decided to teach myself dancing.

10:00 p.m.

Why won't Mum and Dad admit they attacked the caretaker? Why do they insist on lying to me? What else are they hiding from me?

11:00 p.m.

My parents are all right, really. I shouldn't be

so suspicious of them. They're not so bad when it comes down to it.

12:00 a.m.

Why doesn't Chloe love me? Nothing ever goes right in my life. What does anything even mean?

1:00 a.m.

Feeling ill now.

## SUNDAY, FEBRUARY 20

I would like to apologize for the haphazard nature of yesterday's entries. When vampires drink too much blood, it produces a state that is similar to drunkenness in humans.

I have been lying in bed with a thumping head-ache today. It's at times like this that I wish vampires could sleep.

In the future I will be more careful about how much blood I consume. It's said that if vampires regularly drink too much, they become bloodoholics. You used to hear about drifter vampires who lived in a constant state of thirst, becoming too slow and clumsy to hunt and leading a miserable existence sneaking into blood banks through windows. By the time they were caught and destroyed by irate mobs, they were usually relieved.

## MONDAY, FEBRUARY 21

I am feeling better today and have decided to limit myself to three bottles of blood a night.

I went down to the shopping precinct today and sat on a bench. I noticed that a nearby group of older teenagers were smoking, so I asked them to stop, but they refused. I can't believe how antisocial they were. Don't they know they could kill someone with those things? Obviously, they couldn't kill me with them, but they could have damaged the lungs of a human. What if my precious Chloe had been walking past?

I know I wouldn't like it if someone went out in public and did something harmful to me, like throwing holy water and garlic everywhere. If I had vampire speed, I would have snatched their cigarettes and thrown them away in a rapid blur of motion. As it was, I had to make do with tutting and shaking my head, but I think I made my point.

# TUESDAY, FEBRUARY 22
## 10:00 a.m.

Dad told me off this morning for hogging the bathroom when I brush my teeth. He said that vampires don't even need to do it, as our teeth can't decay. That may be true, but I still need to keep my breath minty fresh. After my experience with the deodorant, I'm not taking any chances.

## 1:00 a.m.

If you think your break can be boring, you should try going without sleep for the whole thing.

There's nothing to watch on TV, and I'm stuck at the final level in my current PlayStation game. Welcome to the shadowy, fiendish realm of the undead. I don't think.

I will now try and count up to ten thousand just to pass the time.

2:00 a.m.

I got as far as 148 before I realized how much
I resembled the Count from Sesame Street. I
refuse to conform to these vicious stereotypes.

# WEDNESDAY, FEBRUARY 23

### 8:00 a.m.

How can it only be Wednesday? This break has already felt longer than most summer holidays. What if Chloe has moved again to a different town? What if another boy has stolen her from me while I languish here? What if she's dead? And I don't mean dead in a cool way like me, but actually a dead body.

I must stop torturing myself with these possibilities.

### 7:00 p.m.

I tried to shave my upper lip tonight because I've heard that it makes a mustache grow quicker, so you look older.

I kept cutting my lip and having to wait for it to heal, so I got bored. I don't really want a mustache, anyway, because Dad has one, and it's not cool to look like a miniature version of your parents. In the nineties I had a human friend whose dad used to make the entire family wear matching orange tracksuits. He said it would make it easier for them to find one another in the event of a fire, although why he chose such easily flammable items of clothing for this, I have no idea.

1:00 a.m.
Why did I have to fall in love with a mortal? I am the predator stalking over moonlit hillsides, and she is the sheep for whom I burn.

That last bit came out wrong.

## THURSDAY, FEBRUARY 24
I think something very odd happened to me today, but I'm not sure if I was imagining it. I was

walking down the road to the shopping mall when
a bus full of old people drove past. I caught the
eyes of one of the old ladies in it, and I thought
for a second that she was Caroline Blake, a girl
I used to like in the fifties. As the coach drove
away I tried to work out if it were possible. If

she was fifteen in the early fifties, then I suppose she could be in her seventies now.

I've gotten so used to moving around that I forget humans get older. Since I knew Caroline, she probably got married, had kids, had grandkids, bought a house, moved house, got a job, lost a job, got another job, got ill, got better, and gone gray. And what have I done in all this time? Nothing.

Even my heroic attempt to memorize pi to one hundred places seems trivial and pointless in this light.

## FRIDAY, FEBRUARY 25

The experience that I might or might not have had yesterday has made me realize I have to declare my love to Chloe soon. I can't let her slip away and watch her go past in a busload of old folk in the 2070s. Monday I shall reveal that I'm immortal and announce my everlasting love for her.

On second thought, I might start by asking her to go to the movies with me.

## SATURDAY, FEBRUARY 26

Tomorrow my sister and I will celebrate our transformation day, which is the vampire equivalent of a birthday.

It's celebrated because we're supposed to believe that the day you became a vampire is more important than the day you were born as a human.

We were both transformed in East London on February 27. Mum and Dad fed on our necks until we were weak and then mixed vampire blood into our veins. A few moments later we effectively "died" and then came back to life as vampires. A transformation isn't always a pleasant thing to watch, but then again, neither is human childbirth if we're being honest.

My parents took us from the crowded orphanage where we lived to a comfortable town house, so they've got nothing to feel guilty about. But I still find it arrogant of them to assume that we want to celebrate the end of our human lives. They've been vampires for so long now that all their human memories have gone, but every now and then I still get an echo of how it felt to enjoy a satisfying roast dinner or drift off to sleep with the rain falling on the window.

I haven't forgotten the actual day I was born on, either. It was May 14. This is how I know I'm nearly one hundred years old.

Note to self: One way or another, I must win Chloe's heart before my one hundredth birthday. I can't turn one hundred without having had a girlfriend. That would just be tragic.

## SUNDAY, FEBRUARY 27

My sister came bounding into my room at six this morning to remind me about our transformation day. I don't know why it still thrills her so much. I admit I used to find it exciting, but after a while it begins to serve as a depressing reminder of how long you've been undead and how little you've achieved in that time.

I was quite happy lying around my room and thinking about Chloe, but my sister insisted on dragging me downstairs. For breakfast Mum took out of the fridge a bottle of type AB+ that she'd been saving for a special occasion.

After we drank it, we opened our presents. I got a Fabergé egg, some original Leonardo da Vinci sketches, and a smoking jacket that once belonged to Lord Byron. I would have preferred Guitar Hero, but I made an effort to pretend that I got what I wanted. Mum and Dad are being suspiciously nice to me at the moment. They must be trying to win back my trust after I found out about their attack on the caretaker.

My sister got a Stradivarius violin, a crystal skull, and a ball gown that once belonged to the young

Marie Antoinette. She seemed overjoyed with her presents, although I can't imagine what use she'll make of them. You can bet that skull will be broken this time next week.

I'm back at school tomorrow, and I've promised myself that I'll ask Chloe to go on a date with me.

## MONDAY, FEBRUARY 28

I went back to school today and am happy to report that cruel fate has not yet snatched Chloe from me. I had a good chat with her in the library at lunchtime, although I didn't ask her on a date as I'd promised myself. I think I spent too long talking to her about the questions on fish farming we had to do for science. It wasn't a very romantic topic, in retrospect.

I tried to think of something I did during the

vacation to tell her about, but the only things I could think of were the time I drank too much blood and my transformation day, and that side of my life must remain cloaked for now.

But soon you shall know the truth, flower of the mortal realm.

## TUESDAY, MARCH 1
### 10:00 a.m.
Craig was giving everyone a pinch and a thump this morning, saying, "Pinch, punch, first of the month." I didn't mind because I don't feel pain, but Wayne looked rather angry.

### 1:00 p.m.
Craig has given Susan from our class (who looks like a troll) a note saying that he likes her. Except he hasn't, really, because the note was

a fake written by Wayne to get revenge, and now that Craig has found out, they're going to fight after school. Chloe and I had a chat about how childish all of this behavior is. We have chosen to attend the fight nonetheless.

### 7:00 p.m.

The fight was a disappointment, to say the very least. We all stood around in a circle chanting the word "fight," and then Craig and Wayne pushed each other a bit until Mr. Morris came along and broke it up.

It's times like this when I wish there were still a few vampires around to give us some real entertainment. Although all vampires would face permanent exclusion if they killed one of their own kind, they could formally challenge each other to duels. These duels were epic physical struggles of vampire martial arts that often went on for days and crossed several continents. Which sounds more entertaining than a couple of teenagers shoving each other until a teacher turns up.

After the nonfight, I walked Chloe home for the first time. She lives on Heywood Lane, the nicest street in Stockfield. We could afford to live there if we wanted, but Dad won't spend money on anything because he says it will draw attention to us. Yet he lets Mum hang her ancient ball gowns and corsets on the washing

line where everyone can see them. Could he be any more of a hypocrite?

If you ask me, we're much more likely to draw attention to ourselves living in a semidetached house. If someone with better hearing than Mrs. Perkins ever moves in next door, they might wonder why we stay awake all night, every night.

## WEDNESDAY, MARCH 2

We had a lesson about food chains in science this morning, and it was one of those occasions where I have to keep quiet even though I know the teacher is wrong. Mrs. Jones claimed that humans are "apex predators" because they reside at the top of their food chain. I know this is nonsense because vampires feed on them, so we're the ones who really sit at the top of the food chain. But I managed to keep quiet as she spewed out the misinformation.

I'm still off PE on Wednesday afternoons on account of my imaginary bad back. Whenever I walk past Mr. Jenkins, he really glares at me to see if I'm ill. I know he can't wait for me to go back to his stupid lessons so he can find some new way of humiliating me.

Usually, when I'm feeling angry about a human, I just remind myself that they'll get old and die one day, and then I begin to feel sorry for them. Not in the case of Mr. Jenkins, though. I can feel no pity whatsoever for that fiend.

## THURSDAY, MARCH 3

We had an assembly about global warming today. Apparently, the polar ice caps are melt-ing, and everywhere will be underwater soon. Mrs. Maguire kept going on about how in order to save the planet, we mustn't leave our computers on standby. Why should she care? She'll be dead by then. How does she think I feel? I'm immortal, and I'll be around to see the whole stupid thing. And the worst thing is, I hate swimming.

I wouldn't mind spending eternity on a watery planet with Chloe, though. We could live on a mountain together, and feed on the people swimming past. It would be really romantic.

This afternoon we had fire alarm practice, and Craig sent all the younger students into a frenzy by pretending it was a real fire. I got told off by Mr. Morris for not being quick enough, but I didn't care. A real fire wouldn't do me any lasting damage, anyway, unless somebody accidentally stabbed me with a wooden stake in the panic.

## FRIDAY, MARCH 4

I spent today avoiding Craig because he was showing off his new camera phone and I'm under strict instructions to stay away from cameras.

The idea that vampires don't show up in photographs is just another silly myth, of course. But like many of these misconceptions, it has a basis in truth. Vampires have to stay out of photographs because they make it obvious that we don't age. The last thing you want is for someone to produce a photo of you looking exactly the same twenty years ago.

This is more of a problem for Mum and Dad, as their vampire beauty draws attention even if they're in the very background of a shot. Whereas I'm so instantly forgettable, you could live next door to me for years without noticing that I've always been the same.

Overall, we've been quite good at avoiding photos over the years, but every day it gets harder to duck out of the way of digital cameras, speed cameras, and CCTV. The only bright side is that our mantelpiece isn't cluttered with embar-rassing childhood photos.

## SATURDAY, MARCH 5

Mum is upset with Dad because he never uses the cell phone she bought him. I told her not to buy it, as he always mistrusts new technology. He wouldn't even buy us a washing machine until about twenty years after everyone else had one because he thought it would shrink his capes.

Mum says that she just wants to be able to call him and make sure that he's safe, but I don't know what she thinks is going to happen to him. Unless he falls heart-first onto an upright wooden stake, I doubt he'll be in too much danger.

An update regarding the stupidity of my sister: She has announced that she no longer wishes to kill animals for their blood and will now only consume the blood of animals that have died by accident. Again, she has said she wants to do this on "ethical grounds."

For once, my parents drew a line at her idiocy and refused to cave in. They explained that the blood of dead animals would be stale and make her sick. And how did she react to this sensible advice? By kicking a hole in the kitchen door and stomping off to her room, of course.

I have to say, I'm surprised that they finally put their foot down with her. I expected them to indulge her until it got to the point where she refused to drink anything except the sap of plants.

SUNDAY, MARCH 6

12:00 p.m.

I have come up with a new plan to make Chloe
like me. I shall work out until I force my body to
unleash its vampire strength. I'm off to the gym
right now to put my scheme into action.


5:00 p.m.

Well, that was a massive waste of time. When
I got to the gym, I put the weight machine on
the highest setting and settled down for a
grueling workout. After a couple of fruitless
attempts to move the bars, I was ready to
abandon my plan and go home. Unfortunately,
an assistant who looked like the missing link
between Neanderthal man and PE teacher
stood behind the machine and offered to
"spot" me. He did this by decreasing the load

one level at a time and shouting, "You can do it!"

He was wrong. I couldn't do it. Even when the machine was on the lowest setting, I couldn't do it. I thanked Missing Link for his help and made my shameful exit. Once again, I have my uncooperative body to blame for a humiliating day.

## MONDAY, MARCH 7

Today we had dental checks in the sports hall. I tried to get out of mine by showing the nurse how strong my teeth were, but she wasn't letting anyone off. I think they're trying to catch all the kids whose parents let them have soda and candy.

I was really fretting that my fangs would shame me by extending while the dentist was

examining my teeth.
To keep them under
control, I took
a long sniff of
the garbage cans
they throw the
lunch leftovers in.

In the end,
it wasn't a
problem. The dentist said my teeth were the
strongest and whitest he'd ever seen, although
you could tell he was confused by how cold I was.

He then spent about half an hour looking at
Wayne's mouth and tutting. I'm glad I don't
have potato chips and soda every lunchtime
like him. Say what you like about human blood,
but at least it's natural. What comes out of
the vein goes straight down my throat with

no additives, colorings, or preservatives. I'm quite a health buff when I think about it.

## TUESDAY, MARCH 8
### 12:20 p.m.

Chloe is reading an anthology of Romantic poetry, which contains some by a vampire Dad used to be friends with called Lord Byron. If only she would put the book down and realize that there's someone every bit as brooding and dangerous as Byron right in front of her. And I can also write powerful poetry, just like him.

Why can't Chloe see that I'm just her type?

### 9:00 p.m.

Craig has a pair of Nikes that are black with a black swoosh, so he can get away with wearing them as school shoes. Craig always gets loads of cool stuff because his parents are divorced.

Tonight I asked Dad if I could have a pair, and he said no. I can't believe how tight he is considering his wealth. He always says that we'll draw too much attention to ourselves if we spend lots of money. What he fails to understand is that in this day and age, buying expensive sneakers is normal. It's wearing scuffed old school shoes that's abnormal now. Social services would take me away if they saw the rags I'm forced to wear.

If he doesn't buy me some cooler clothes soon, I'll get teased like Darren and nobody will ever sit next to me again.

## WEDNESDAY, MARCH 9

Everyone was sniggering and looking at me in expectation as I sat down in math this morning. It took me a while to realize that Craig had put a thumbtack on my chair. I had to pretend it hurt just to get them to stop looking at me and move on to the next victim.

In the library at lunchtime, Chloe asked me what my political views were, but I couldn't think of any. I remember Mr. Morris once saying that vampires are capitalists or capitalists are vampires or something, so I said I was a capitalist. Chloe didn't seem very impressed. I think I need to find a more interesting "ist."

On TV tonight there was a murder mystery set in the twenties, but they didn't get many details right. The vast majority of us didn't swan around in country houses, waiting to be murdered by butlers, we just got on with our lives. Although there was less technology, life wasn't that different, really. Declaring your love to a girl is just as difficult, whether you do it by handwritten letter or e-mail, and my sister is just as annoying whether she's learning the Charleston or hip-hop dancing.

I've just had a strange thought. The twenties will be coming back round again soon! Mum and Dad must be used to this kind of thing now, but I'm not even one hundred yet, so it's all still a novelty to me.

## THURSDAY, MARCH 10
## 8:00 a.m.

Mum has washed my school shirt with one of Dad's capes, and it's turned pink! I told her that the red lining of his capes would ruin everything, but she wouldn't listen. She wanted me to wear one of Dad's shirts to school, but they've all got ridiculous frilly bits. I'm not going to school dressed as Duran Duran!

## 10:00 a.m.

I made Mum drive me to the store to get a shirt on the way to school, and we had to bang on the door to make them open it early. Mum complained the whole time, but this is what she gets for putting my school clothes in with Dad's outlandish garb.

## 9:00 p.m.

I sat next to Chloe in art today, and she had a sniffle. It's weird, but if my sister had a sniffle, it would drive me over the edge. Yet when Chloe has one, it sounds like a gentle breeze blowing through rose petals. I am truly beginning to understand the power of love.

At lunchtime Wayne was going round with a sponsorship form for a fun run he's doing for endangered species. I kept out of his way so I didn't have to pledge anything. Why should I? Vampires are an endangered species, but nobody ever runs for us. They run from us, but that's not the same.

## 4:00 a.m.

They never put anything decent on TV at this time. It's really unfair on shift workers and the undead. I suppose I should be grateful that they show anything at all during the night. Believe it or not, it was only a few years ago that they used to play the national anthem and tell you to go to bed before midnight. And a few years before that, there was no TV at all. No wonder so many vampires got up to mischief in the old days. They had nothing else to do!

## FRIDAY, MARCH 11

Craig was told off by the principal for wearing his cool sneakers today. You should have heard him complaining about it. All they said was that he had to wear school shoes on Monday or he'd get detention.

In the old days they used to whack you with a cane or leather strap if you did the slightest thing wrong. I was once hit with a slipper just for walking too fast in the corridor. Not that Dad had any sympathy when I told him. He just went on about the time he was tortured on a rack for whistling during longbow practice. Whatever I tell him, he always has to try and top it.

## SATURDAY, MARCH 12

I was bored tonight so I went for a walk in the graveyard. I realize that makes me sound like a vampire cliché, but it's the only place where I can go to be quiet and relax on a Saturday night. Everywhere else is full of people fighting and throwing up on one another.

As I lurked moodily around

the tombs, I heard human voices in the distance. I followed them and realized that John, Si, and

Brian had come to the graveyard too. I thought I'd scare them for a joke, so I rushed out from behind a grave.

They let out shrieks of fear and dashed toward the exit, which was very cowardly for people who claim to be hard-core horror fanatics. I was surprised to see them running so fast, especially Brian, who certainly never moves like that on sports day. They made such a speedy exit that I didn't get the chance to reveal that it was only me.

The weird thing was, as I raced after them to explain that it was all a prank, it sort of stopped being one. I really did feel like pouncing on them and drinking their blood.

I think the moral of this episode is that if you're going to pretend to be a blood-drinking supernatural being, make sure you're not actually a blood-drinking supernatural being, or you could get carried away.

## SUNDAY, MARCH 13
6:00 p.m.

We all went out for a family hike again today. As usual, Dad drove his Volvo well over the speed limit. He says that his supernatural vampire speed makes it hard for him to drive as slowly as a human, but I think this is just an excuse. He needs to be careful. He could end up in prison for speeding, and then I'd be from a broken home like Darren.

I've never understood why Dad buys Volvos. He says they've got strong frames that don't buckle in crashes, but why should we care? We could drive off the edge of a cliff and land in a fireball and we'd all be fine again after ten minutes. Still, at least it stops him from buying a sports car and becoming a complete embarrassment.

## 9:00 p.m.

I've found out what "ist" I am—an anarchist! I saw a politician on TV tonight saying that if we don't spend more on policing, society will break down into lawless anarchy and blood will run in the streets. Sounds brilliant!

## MONDAY, MARCH 14

Craig wore his normal school shoes again today, but as a protest he has written his persuasive writing essay for English about how we shouldn't have any school uniform at all. I suppose I should agree now that I'm an anarchist.

When I told Chloe, she said he'd been very mature to use his essay as a protest rather than simply writing it about capital punishment like the teacher suggested. I agreed with her wholeheartedly and hid my capital punishment essay under my folder.

I was worried that John, Si, and Brian might have started the rumor that there are vampires in town after my misjudged prank on Saturday night. I need to be very careful not to fuel this kind of gossip, given my parents' reckless attack on the school caretaker. Fortunately, my Goth friends are far too stupid to have understood what was going on, and they've been boasting about how they banished a specter from the graveyard instead. Now everyone is chanting the *Ghostbusters* theme at them, and I have no sympathy.

### TUESDAY, MARCH 15

The English teacher liked Craig's essay so much, she showed it to the principal in the staff room.

The principal said that Craig had been very assertive to write an argument against the rules rather than simply breaking them. He said that he couldn't go as far as to abolish school uniforms, but that as a gesture of goodwill, he would let us have a No Uniform Day on Friday if we all give a pound to charity.

Everyone is looking forward to it except for Darren, who only owns his school uniform and PE uniform, and is so poor that he should be receiving charity money rather than donating it. At

first I was pleased about Craig's moral victory,
but I soon began to worry that none of my
clothes were cool enough.

When I got home, I had to go on at Mum and
Dad for ages to get
some money for new
clothes. Dad said I
could wear something
from his wardrobe if
I wanted. I told him
it was No Uniform
Day, not Halloween.
I even threatened
to run away from
home, but I've been saying this for over eighty
years, so it doesn't have much effect now. In
the end, they coughed up a measly forty pounds,
which is barely enough to buy some jeans and

a T-shirt. When I mentioned to Mum that I was going to spend it in the Goth shop in the precinct, she even asked me to get her some candles out of the same money! They need to understand that prices have gone up since the nineteenth century.

## WEDNESDAY, MARCH 16

Today I found out that my parents have attacked another person here in town! I was in the Goth shop, and I heard one of the assistants talking about how he'd been ill for a couple of days and was still feeling "seriously weak." I went to the cash register and got a good look at his neck. Sure enough, there were a couple of holes right over the jugular.

When I told Mum and Dad about it, they said I must have made a mistake and that the holes were probably just a novelty tattoo, but I know vampire bite marks when I see them. Either they're liars, or they're getting so overcome by their desires that they don't even know they're doing it anymore.

If they must feed on someone in town, they

could hardly pick a worse victim than the assistant from the Goth store. If a normal human remembers something about the experience afterward, they'll assume they're having flashbacks to a nightmare. But as Goths believe in vampires, they'll have no problem accepting it and blabbing to their friends about how there's a coven in town. Before we know it, we'll have a huge line of idiots in top hats, frilly shirts, and capes banging on our front door and begging to be transformed.

Needless to say, we'd have to move to another town, and I'd be forced to leave my soul mate Chloe behind forever. It would be utterly unbearable.

I told Mum and Dad very firmly to stop snacking on local people willy-nilly, and slammed the door to emphasize my point.

# THURSDAY, MARCH 17

1:00 p.m.

According to Craig, the kids from the toughest school in town are coming round after school to steal our phones and beat us up. Everyone is really scared.

7:00 p.m.

Nothing happened after school. Craig was just winding us all up. Everyone pretended that they didn't fall for it, but they really did. I have to admit, even I got swept along in the wave of hysteria.

Why am I so pathetic? I'm supposed to be an ancient and deadly creature of the night. Why was I getting worried about a bunch of kids who wear tracksuits and baseball caps?

I am refusing to speak to Mum and Dad until they own up to the attacks on the caretaker and the shop assistant. How can they expect me to be open with them when they tell such blatant lies?

The most infuriating thing about all of this is that I only found out about these attacks by chance, so I dread to think how many others they've kept hidden from me. And if they find it so easy to deceive me on this matter, what else are they keeping me in the dark about?

I know I sound paranoid, but this is what I've been driven to.


2:00 a.m.

Mum and Dad wouldn't let me have any blood unless I started speaking to them again. I was thirsty, so I had to give in to their demands, but I told them I will be treating everything they say from now on with the utmost suspicion.

## FRIDAY, MARCH 18

I wore my new black jeans and shirt from the Goth shop to No Uniform Day. I looked quite cool, but my scuffed old shoes let my outfit down.

Chloe looked like a bit of a Goth herself in a black T-shirt and a long black skirt, which I took as further proof that I'm just her type, although she doesn't quite realize it yet.

Craig wore an expensive pair of white air-cushioned sneakers rather than the ones that started the whole uniform controversy in the first place. Surprise of the day, though, was Darren, who wore a tracksuit bearing a proper brand name rather than the word "sport."

When I commented on this curious turn of events to Chloe, she confessed that the tracksuit actually belonged to her father and that she'd secretly lent it to Darren so he wouldn't get teased. She is so caring and selfless. From now on I will try to think more about the needs of others rather than my own. That way she'll be more likely to let me drink her blood.

## SATURDAY, MARCH 19

This morning was rainy, so I went for a walk in the park. I like going out in bad weather, because I don't feel the cold and I get the park to myself. I didn't quite get the relaxing stroll I was hoping for, though.

As I entered the gates I noticed several

squirrels
standing
on their
back legs
and baring their teeth. I
suppose it should have looked odd to me, but I'm
used to this kind of thing. All animals hate me.
Dogs growl at me, cats hiss and arch their backs,
and I'm sure I've heard pigeons coo aggressively
once or twice.

So, I thought nothing when I saw a group
of squirrels glaring at me as I went about my
morning stroll. I wasn't really concentrating on
them because I was thinking about Chloe, so I
didn't notice when the nasty things surrounded
me. They blocked the path ahead of me, and
when I glanced behind me, I saw hundreds of
them there, too. Before I knew it, the vile

creatures were jumping on me and scratching me with their tiny claws. As I ripped them off and threw them to the ground, more came forward. It was only when I ran out of the park that the foul vermin ceased their attack and returned to standing on their back legs and glaring.

I've heard of vampires being attacked by packs of wolves and snakes before, but never a load of mangy squirrels. Why does it always happen to me?

# SUNDAY, MARCH 20

## 2:00 p.m.

I didn't want to go outside again after yesterday's attack. I don't know if I'm being paranoid, but I think word has gotten round the animal kingdom that there's a vampire who is too weak to fight back, and now they can all get their revenge on my kind.

If you believe the stories, they've got plenty to get revenge for. Dad once told me that a vampire sneaked onto Noah's ark and chomped his way through hundreds of now extinct species, including the seven-headed snake and the multicolored panda. I used to believe Dad's stories, but now I think they're to be taken with a pinch of salt.

He also says that some vampires could mesmerize animals such as dogs and cats and use them to attack enemies. I'm not convinced that it ever really happened, but I know that many dogs and cats were accused of consorting with the undead and banished from towns in the great vampire purges of the nineteenth century, so they've still got good reason to hold a grudge.

9:00 p.m.

My parents want me to play the piano for them, but I don't feel like doing anything for those liars. I used to quite enjoy family music nights, but I don't often find myself in the mood anymore. And my dad always makes the same joke of saying, "The children of the night, what music they make," in the style of Bela Lugosi from the old film of Dracula.

I'll stick to my PlayStation, thank you very much.

# MONDAY, MARCH 21

Craig lent me a new game today where you have to shoot zombies. It's supposed to be for people over seventeen, so Dad wouldn't let me buy it, even though I'm more than five times that age. It was quite a spooky game with atmospheric music, although it spoils the effect if you know that zombies couldn't do much harm to you even if they were real. I'd like to see one of that shambolic lot try and ram a stake through my heart.

I glanced in my sister's room this evening and caught her acting out a vampire scene with her Ken and Barbie dolls. She'd fashioned a cape for Ken out of a candy wrapper and a couple of fangs using the ends of toothpicks, and she was making him chase after Barbie and feed on her neck. I watched her for ages before she spotted me. When she did, she got angry and slammed the door so hard it came off its hinges, so Mum and Dad made me fix it as a punishment.

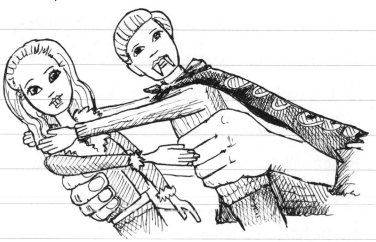

I can't believe Mum and Dad punished me for something my sister did wrong! I would have complained if I felt I was dealing with rational and intelligent beings.

### TUESDAY, MARCH 22

We're having a Parents' Evening on Thursday and I'm dreading it. I know Mum and Dad will do something embarrassing. I think I'll ask them to sign the form that says they're staying away, like Darren's mum does.

I gave Craig his zombie game back today as I've already completed it on hard mode. He was very impressed by how quickly I did it, and it made me wonder if I do have vampire powers after all, but only for computer games. I'm sure the extra eight hours a night gaming time I get because I don't sleep has something to do with it, though.

We're supposed to analyze an article in a newspaper as our homework for media studies, but I forgot to buy one, and the only papers I could find in Dad's study were ancient and yellow. I think it would confuse everyone if I did my homework about how the *Times* covered the sinking of the *Titanic*.

## WEDNESDAY, MARCH 23

Luckily, the media studies teacher was off sick today, so it didn't matter that I hadn't done my homework. Even better, an old retired teacher called Mr. Pilkington came in to cover, and he said that media wasn't a proper subject and we were all wasting our time. He said that we didn't get taught properly these days and that he was going to give us an hour of real education for once. He then spent the lesson asking us about the British Empire. I was the only one who knew the answers, because we used to do all that stuff in school fifty years ago. Mr. Pilkington said that I was the only true patriot in the class, and I felt really proud. But then I got worried that I would get beaten up for being a brain, so I shut up.

I am totally dreading Parents' Evening

tomorrow. I hope Chloe doesn't see us and realize what a family of freaks I'm from.

## THURSDAY, MARCH 24

Mum and Dad came to Parents' Evening wearing
really embarrassing clothes. Dad wore a velvet
suit and frilly shirt from the nineteenth century,
and Mum wore a ball gown from prerevolutionary
France. For all the attempts

at blending in they made, they might as well have turned up in a pumpkin carriage drawn by bats.

On the other hand, their supernatural allure did at least inspire my teachers to paper over some of the weaker aspects of my performance. Mr. Wilson clearly took a shine to Mum and said that I applied myself very well in math, even though I got eleven out of twenty correct on the last test, and that was only because I'd done it before. Mr. Morris said that my work in history was excellent, even if I sometimes embellished it with imaginary details about what life was like in the early twentieth century. Even Mrs. Bowles said I was a joy to have around in home ec class. A joy to have around? I spend every lesson on the verge of throwing up into one of the garbage cans as the food smells assault my nostrils. I couldn't be less of a joy to have around if I dragged my nails down the blackboard for the entire hour.

I made a big effort to keep Mum and Dad away from the gym where Mr. Jenkins and the PE staff were grunting through their meetings. The last thing I needed was for Dad to let it slip that I'm not really ill, and put me back at the mercy of that torturer. As we were leaving I saw Mr. Jenkins standing on the gym fire escape staring at us with great interest, so I herded them quickly away.

I'd forgotten about the hypnotic effect Mum and Dad have on humans. Maybe I should introduce them to Chloe and see if their mesmeric attraction extends to me by association.

## FRIDAY, MARCH 25

We were watching a DVD called _Life During Wartime_ in history today, and guess who turned up in it? I did! And so did the rest of my family!

There was an archive clip showing how children had to go and live in the countryside during World War II, and you could clearly make us out in the corner of the frame. We're usually good at avoiding cameras, but we must have missed that one.

I hope nobody spots this and works out we're immortal. We'll end up getting driven out of our home by irate townsfolk. Plus, I still owe a considerable library fine in the last town we lived in, and I wouldn't want that to catch up with me.

It didn't look like anyone in the class noticed, though I couldn't help but wonder if I saw a slight look of confusion on Chloe's face. Is she beginning to suspect my true nature?

## SATURDAY, MARCH 26
## 1:00 p.m.
I have bought a book called *The Secrets of Success with Women*. It must contain very powerful secrets as the man on the cover has terrible hair and looks really sleazy. The techniques must be powerful if they helped him.

## 6:00 p.m.
I have finished the book now, but it didn't contain any secrets. It just said that you have

to make eye contact, smile a lot, and touch women's arms when you talk to them. I've heard this kind of advice bandied about for over eight decades now, and it's easier said than done. Also, the author made several stupid generaliza-tions about dating in the past, a subject that he can't possibly know about. He said that it's harder to find girls now than it was in the six-ties. Well, I lived through the sixties, and take it from me, it was just as impossible to approach girls back then.

### SUNDAY, MARCH 27

My parents announced that we'd be going on a family hike today, and I foolishly agreed to join them. They took it upon themselves to dash up a rocky slope, and I attempted to follow.

I misplaced my footing, fell hundreds of feet down, and broke my arm. It was really annoying and took almost five minutes to heal.

Obviously, as a vampire, I can't really be harmed unless someone chops my head off or rams a stake into my heart, but I can still get temporarily injured. I was hit by a car in the eighties, and I broke so many bones it took me almost twenty minutes to recover. I was inside an ambulance by then, and I had to wait until it stopped at the lights to run away. The whole situation was incredibly embarrassing, and it certainly made me think twice about crossing the road without looking.

At least I've never had a really serious accident, though. They say that Roderick of Colchester lost all his limbs in the Battle of Balaclava, and it took a week for his severed arms and legs to crawl their way across the battlefield and reattach themselves. It must have been a real hassle.

On the way back to the car we passed a group of hikers who were really staring at us. I wish Dad wouldn't wear his cape when we go hiking.

### MONDAY, MARCH 28
#### 10:00 a.m.

In assembly today, the principal revealed the destination of our year's school trip next week.

It isn't very good news for me since we're going to the zoo!

As animals hate me, a place filled with them is unlikely to be a suitable destination. Why do I have to get all the bad things about being a vampire, but none of the good things? I hate my life.

Pretty much any other school trip would have been better for me. Unless World of Garlic, Crucifixes, and Vampire Slayers amusement park exists. But I know that if I stay behind, another boy will sit next to Chloe on the bus. I simply have to go, and the animals are just going to have to put up with it.


6:00 p.m.

We had a drama lesson this afternoon, and I was in a group with Si and Brian the Goths.

152

We had to devise a short piece to perform for the rest of the class, and Si suggested that we do it about vampires. He came up with a really corny idea about us emerging from coffins in a graveyard and boasting about the people we were going to bite. It was really inaccurate, and most of it was stolen from the vampire TV show they watch, but I couldn't be bothered arguing, so I went along with it.

We performed our piece to the group, and Si and Brian put on hammy Eastern European accents. What is it with these Eastern European accents everyone does when they pretend to be vampires? In the days before the vampire purges, there were covens in places as far apart as New Orleans, Paris, Alaska, Stockholm, and Santa Carla. Admittedly, there was a coven in Transylvania, but it was by no means the only one.

After our piece, the drama teacher, Mrs. Stokes, said that it was good overall but that I didn't put in as much effort as Si and Brian!

This is so humiliating. I know I make a less convincing vampire than my parents, but I didn't expect to make a less convincing vampire than a pair of Goths!

## TUESDAY, MARCH 29

Today I hung around with the tough gang and won some street cred. Bet you weren't expecting that, were you?

Jay and Baz from the tough gang were making everyone play a game called Mercy, where you have to link fingers with someone else and then press forward with your wrists until the other person says "mercy." Jay grabbed me as I was on my way to the library and said I had to play. He expected that I would give up and scream for mercy in seconds like everyone else he had been terrorizing, but I didn't even wince as he bent my palms back. Unfortunately, I didn't have the strength to mount a counterattack, either, so we just stood there for a couple of minutes like we were holding hands. Eventually Jay gave up and put his hands

155

down, and Baz said that under the rules of Mercy, I was the winner.

Jay said I was "all right" and "not as bad as the other weirdos," and I gratefully accepted his compliment. Word of my astonishing victory soon traveled around the school, and in some versions of the story, I even made him beg for mercy. The stories made me sound really heroic, and I hoped they would reach Chloe's ears.

## WEDNESDAY, MARCH 30
## 4:00 p.m.

Mr. Jenkins is getting on my case about my continuing absence from PE. He came to the library at lunchtime and harassed me. He asked me if I was coming to his lesson today, and I said I wasn't. He really boomed the question out, probably because he's never been in a library before and doesn't know you're supposed to be quiet. He then touched his hand to my forehead and admitted that I felt cold and unwell. Thank you, vampire temperature, for getting me out of another miserable PE afternoon!

Mr. Jenkins walked away, but he kept shooting suspicious glances back at me. You can tell he really hates me. If I ever have to attend another one of his lessons, it's going to be awful. I must think of a better long-term strategy to escape him.

2:00 a.m.

Craig has loaned me a new PlayStation game,
but I didn't realize until I started playing that
it's about vampires. I've been playing it for a
few hours now, and I'm really bored. I'm worse
than those people who drive home from work and
immediately start playing driving games.

## THURSDAY, MARCH 31
1:00 p.m.

I intended to take my usual seat next to Chloe
in art today. However, when I arrived, I noticed
that Wayne was already sitting there.

To make things worse, the only seat left
was next to Darren, and it's common knowledge
that you'll get fleas if you sit next to him. In
the end I had to construct a flea-proof barrier
between us with an easel.

158

I started to get worried about Wayne as I watched him sitting next to Chloe. But I doubt Chloe would have been impressed by his artistic skills. All he ever does is draw pictures of the tattoos he wants.

6:00 p.m.

Mum and Dad have been out hunting, and they've brought back some lovely type-O blood. Dad tried to tell me about the man he'd siphoned it from, but I didn't want to know. It always puts me off to find out about the people blood comes from. This is another reason why I don't want Mum and Dad to hunt in this town. Nothing is more likely to make me lose my appetite than finding out the blood I'm drinking came from the sweaty bloke who works in the all-night garage.

Dad's very old-fashioned about who he feeds on, and he still follows the hierarchy of victims laid out by the Vampire Council, which commands that you snack on people according to their status in society. So, for example, you can feed on a laborer whenever you feel like it, you can only feed on a merchant when you're ravenous, and you can never feed on a king.

It's a really silly and old-fashioned system, which lists "apothecaries," "costermongers," and "falconers," but not computer programmers and call center workers, and it's based on the sort of class system that our history teacher, Mr. Morris, gets angry about.

In fact, the whole thing is completely unjust, and if I think about it for a moment longer it's going to put me off this lovely blood that I'm currently enjoying.

## FRIDAY, APRIL 1

Today I asked Chloe to be my girlfriend, and she agreed. I sank my teeth into her neck and drank from her jugular in the library at lunch-time. She's agreed to join me as a vampire, and she's moving in next week.

April fool!

All joking aside, I expect to be referring to Chloe as my girlfriend in all seriousness soon, as I'm planning to declare my love to her during the school trip.

## SATURDAY, APRIL 2

I went out for a walk around town this after-noon, and I ended up going past the old people's home. I know I sometimes complain about how boring immortality can get, but I'm glad I'm not going to get old. They all looked so bored staring out of the window and nodding off.

Perhaps I should stop moaning about my life and appreciate the good things about it. I'll never go bald, I'll never get fat, and I'll never develop a taste for chunky knitwear. Plus, I'll have a girlfriend for the very first time as soon as I get round to asking Chloe out. All in all, things are looking up.

## SUNDAY, APRIL 3

I went downstairs to get some blood from the fridge this afternoon, and I saw Mum and Dad cuddling on the sofa. It was so disgusting, I nearly lost my appetite. You'd think that after two hundred years of marriage, the spark would have gone out, but they're still all over each other.

I think part of the reason why Dad appreciates Mum so much is that he had so many problems with vampire women in the past.

One of his ex-girlfriends was a psychic vampire who kept getting in bad moods with him over fights they hadn't even had yet, and she even locked him out of the house for forgetting their next anniversary. In the end, she came right out and told him that he was going to split up with her and that she didn't want to see him again.

Another of his ex-girlfriends was both telepathic and a constant nagger. If she wanted him to put up some shelves or clean the house, she'd repeat the message in his brain for hours on end. Even when he went out, he couldn't escape it.

But worst of all Dad's ex-girlfriends was the one who had mind-control powers. Dad said that he would often come round in a daze and find himself buying her an expensive gift. He couldn't even relax at a wrestling or boxing match without being struck by the urge to go home and have a cozy night in.

After all that hassle, it must have been a relief to go out with a normal vampire.

## MONDAY, APRIL 4

We've all got to be at school by eight thirty tomorrow morning so we can get on the bus for the zoo trip. I'm going to get there at eight to make sure no one else sits next to Chloe.

I will offer Chloe the window seat, to show to her how selfless and caring I am. I shall even buy some of that candy she likes.

Tomorrow's going to be good for me. I can sense it.

## TUESDAY, APRIL 5

Let's just say that the school trip wasn't a resounding success.

As we got on the bus I made sure I was sitting next to Chloe. I could see Wayne wanted to barge in, but I didn't let him. Chloe and I had a good chat on the journey there, and

165

I demonstrated my maturity by resisting the temptation to laugh when the bus went past a tramp and Craig told Darren to wave at his dad.

Anyway, we had a nice enough journey, but the zoo itself was a disaster. As soon as I stepped through the turnstile, I could hear yelps of panic coming from the cages. I asked Chloe to hang back with me, so we could break away from the other kids.

The first animals we passed were the meer-kats, who all stood on their hind legs and nudged each other disapprovingly. Next, we walked past a lion that retreated to the back of its cage and roared obnoxiously at me. But it was the monkeys that really drew attention to me. As I passed them, they formed into a threatening rank and howled at me. They threw rocks from their enclosure with scary precision, hitting my head a few times. I tried to pretend it wasn't happening, but it became harder to shrug off when the little monsters began to hurl themselves with great force against their cage. By this point frightened yelps and howls were coming from every direction and an angry zookeeper threw me out for provoking the animals. I hadn't even done anything!

I ended up waiting in the bus on my own while Chloe spent the day with Wayne! And they sat together on the way back! I can only hope that the smell of the cages put him off asking her out in the zoo.

Just when I thought things couldn't get any worse, I found that Craig had spread the rumor that the monkeys threw their poo at me and I ran away in tears. Why couldn't we just have gone to the science museum like last year?

## WEDNESDAY, APRIL 6

It's amazing how quickly you can become a social outcast. Just a week ago I was riding high in the popularity stakes following my Mercy victory over Jay from the tough gang. Now, everywhere I go, I'm greeted by mocking laughter and cruel jibes. Overnight my very name has become an insult. I know this because I heard a kid I've never spoken to saying, "Don't be such a Nigel" in the corridor this morning.

At break time I saw that an obscene picture had been taped to my locker. It depicted me crying. The picture was unsigned, but from the crude style, I'd say the perpetrator was Wayne.

Chloe wasn't in the library at lunchtime, but I decided to sit there on my own rather than look for her. I have no desire to drag her into the scandal.

Resigned to my social failure,

NIGEL LIKES MONKEY POO

I deliberately chose to sit next to Darren in math this afternoon. But guess what? This time he built a barrier out of textbooks to block me out. Even that social outcast considers me persona non grata.

## THURSDAY, APRIL 7

Today I tried to explain to everyone that the monkeys had thrown rocks, but they wouldn't listen. I tried to tell Craig, but he made monkey noises every time I opened my mouth. I even tried to explain it to the girls from the popular gang, but they ran away whenever I went near.

Once again Chloe was absent from the library at lunchtime. Perhaps she is worried about becoming a social outcast if she's seen with me.

# FRIDAY, APRIL 8

My life is over.

Yesterday at lunchtime, Wayne asked Chloe out and she said yes. Unconfirmed reports suggest that they've already been spotted holding hands between classes.

As soon as I heard the news, I went home. It is now approaching nightfall, and I'm still too upset to write anything more. If these words are hard to read, it's probably because I've smudged them with bitter tears.

I have faced many challenges and setbacks in my time on this planet, but this latest blow is too much. I am simply too sensitive for this world.

## SATURDAY, APRIL 9

It is now the Easter holidays. I have a couple of weeks off to try and process what has happened.

How am I going to get through the days?

How am I going to survive?

I know that great art can come from great heartbreak, so I will try and express my feelings in a poem when I have the strength to write more.

## SUNDAY, APRIL 10

I have now written my heartbreak poem. It is very deep and moving, and contains old-fashioned words like "doth." It was very difficult to put my pain into words, but at least it means that

mankind will be able to look back and understand the true depth of my feelings.

## MY LOVE HAS BEEN STOLEN
My love has been stolen
And I am in hell
Now in my heart
Nightmares doth dwell
My love has been stolen
And I am in grief
How could she forsake me
For a boy with bad teeth?

## MONDAY, APRIL 11
I am too upset to drink blood. This lunchtime
Dad noticed that I hadn't touched the bottle
he brought to my room yesterday and asked if
anything was wrong. Like, duh! Earth to Dad!

My life fell apart on Friday, and it's taken him this long to work out that something is wrong.

Of course, I told him nothing. He wouldn't understand, anyway. He's never had any problems attracting women.

God, I hate him. Sometimes I wish he'd never transformed me.

## TUESDAY, APRIL 12

I went for a walk in the countryside today and spent a couple of hours looking over the edge of a cliff. I wanted to end it all by jumping off, but then I remembered that it wouldn't really end anything.

No matter how many bones I broke, I'd only lie on the floor until my body mended and then I'd have to get up and continue my miserable existence.

The only thing I'd really be putting at risk

would be my phone, which would get crushed, and then I'd have to go back to using my old one, which doesn't have a color screen.

It wouldn't even hurt, as I don't feel pain. But I make up for this with the emotional pain I feel, which is the worst anyone has ever experienced in history.

## WEDNESDAY, APRIL 13

When you think about it, it's not very easy for a vampire to end it all. Even if you had the strength, it would be hard to drive a stake through your own heart, and beheading yourself would be tricky.

Dad once told me that the Archduchess of Austria managed to chop her own head off on a guillotine when Aldric of Lyon left her for a younger vampire during the French Revolution, but this is probably just another one of his tall tales.

I once saw a jar of garlic capsules in a health food shop and wondered if I would die if I washed the lot down with holy water. I don't really want to try, though. I'll probably just get the worst migraine in vampire history. And my sister will choose that exact moment to blast out her teen pop at full volume.

No, I have no choice but to navigate this eternal river of loneliness in a boat of solitude.

Note to self: I must remember to include this powerful image in a poem.

## THURSDAY, APRIL 14
## 8:00 a.m.

There's only a month to go until I turn one hundred. I can't believe I'm nearly one hundred and

I haven't even fed on a girl's neck yet. Most vampires have done it loads of times when they reach that age.

## 12:00 A.M.

My parents suggested that we go for a family hike today. Needless to say, I refused. In the end they went off without me, saying that I didn't know what I was missing.

I do know what I'm missing—the point of existence.

## 2:00 A.M.

I once read that a huge asteroid is going to destroy the world in a few hundred years. I'm willing it to hurry up, but I've got a suspicion that even the destruction of the world won't kill me. I'll just end up floating aimlessly around space for the rest of eternity. It won't be that different from my current life, when you think about it.

## FRIDAY, APRIL 15

How could this cruel universe let me get so close to happiness and then snatch it from me?

It is like glimpsing a rainbow only to be condemned to darkness. It is like hearing beautiful music only to be condemned to silence. It is like

smelling sweet rose petals before being condemned to math-teacher breath.

I am truly at rock bottom.

SATURDAY, APRIL 16

11:00 a.m.

The hair I tape over my diary to make sure no
one opens it has been broken!

I am so angry with my sister! I know she is the
culprit because no one else has been in our house
and my parents are too self-absorbed to care
about what I'm going through. I am absolutely
fuming. As soon as Mum and Dad go out hunting
tonight, I intend to confront her.

11:00 p.m.

I would like to make a correction. When I wrote
yesterday that I was at rock bottom, I got it

179

wrong. I have just been beaten up by my little sister. Now I am at rock bottom.

When Mum and Dad went out, I dashed into her room and told her that I knew she'd been reading my diary. At first she denied it, but when I told her about the hair, she had no choice but to confess. She said she'd only looked at it for a couple of minutes, anyway, because it was really boring.

I know that, as a child, she can hardly be expected to understand the depth of emotion I deal with in these pages, but I must admit that this criticism sent me into a violent rage and I attempted to strike her.

As I've previously mentioned, my sister has all the mighty speed and strength expected of vampires, so she easily caught my hand, twisted

it behind my back, and slammed me into a head-
lock. She held me in this
position until I prom-
ised not to lash
out again and
admitted that
my real name
was "Mr. Smellypants."

You might have won this one, little fiend. But
I shall never forget this mistreatment.

## SUNDAY, APRIL 17

The only positive thing to come from my recent
experiences is that I'm writing poetry of even
greater intensity than before. My poems are
now getting so profound, they don't even
rhyme.

# THE HUNTER

If I am the biter, why am I bitten?

If I am the attacker, why am I attacked?

If I am the hunter, why am I hunted

By despair?

In the future, scholars will look back on this period as a great time for my art. But that doesn't matter to me. I write poetry to express myself, and I don't care what anyone else thinks about it.

Note to self: Look into possibility of getting poems published.

# MONDAY, APRIL 18

I ventured out of the house today to try and get some air, but I soon wished I hadn't when

I saw Wayne and Chloe waiting together at the bus stop. They were getting the number 32 to the mall, perhaps to go bowling, see a movie, or get a pizza.

And while they enjoy the taste of mozzarella, pepperoni, and cheese-filled crusts, I shall taste only bitter despair. With an extra topping of depression.

(Note to self: Look into possibility of bequeathing diary to the British Library. These insights into heartbreak must not be lost.)

Perhaps I should leave town. Mum and Dad reckon we're the last vampires left, but I bet there are still some other undead families they don't know about in places like Sweden and Alaska.

Or maybe I'll be killed by a vampire slayer, and then my poetry will be discovered and the world will realize what it's lost. Too late, world. You should have appreciated me when you had the chance.

## TUESDAY, APRIL 19

I popped out to buy the new issue of my computer games magazine this morning and I heard an old lady complaining about a recent illness at the newsstand. It sounded suspicious, so I took a close look at her neck and, sure enough, there were a couple of bite marks right above the collar of her blouse.

I can't believe my parents have been up to their tricks yet again! They are insatiable! It's difficult enough coping with a broken heart without having to worry about an angry mob driving a stake through it because they've discovered my true identity. And all because my parents cannot be bothered to go farther afield to hunt for me. They are so lazy.

As usual, they denied everything when I confronted them this evening, but who else could have done it?

## WEDNESDAY, APRIL 20

I was scared to go out today in case I saw Wayne and Chloe again. It would simply be more than I could stand to see that rotten-toothed fool parading around with the only girl I have ever loved. But I couldn't face another day of staring at my wall, either, so I went to the shopping center and sat on a bench. An old man stood next to me and said he could see I was troubled. At least somebody noticed!

He asked me what the problem was, but when I started to tell him, it didn't take long for him to twist the conversation to the subject of Jesus. I looked up and saw that he was handing out flyers for the local church youth group. His crucifix pendant was dangling right in my face, so now I've got a horrible migraine as well as severe depression. I think I'll stay in tomorrow.

## THURSDAY, APRIL 21

Today was so pointless that when I tried to write about it a moment ago, my pen ran out because it couldn't take the boredom. It took me ages to find a new one, and after all that effort I can exclusively reveal that nothing interesting happened today.

I stayed in bed this morning, and this afternoon I went for a walk and kicked over a traffic cone in anger. A moment later I started feeling guilty and went back to put it upright again. How pathetic. I'm supposed to be a prince of darkness, and I can't even overturn a traffic cone.

Another brilliant day, then.


NOTE: I was being ironic in that last statement. Thought I might need to point that out in case my sister steals my diary and reads it again.


## FRIDAY, APRIL 22

I have written a new poem today. I will let it speak for itself.

# THE PREDATOR

I am the predator
Who wants to suck your blood.
So how can it be that
You sucked the life from me
With rejection?
It sucks.

## SATURDAY, APRIL 23

Today is St. George's Day. There's an ancient superstition that vampires are most active on St. George's Day. I was a pretty good argument against it today; I did nothing but stare at my bedroom ceiling and reflect on how I've ruined my life.

## SUNDAY, APRIL 24

Now it is Easter Sunday, where everyone makes

a big deal about somebody who came back from the dead two thousand years ago.

And what about me? I came back from the dead much more recently than that, but nobody seems interested. Oh, that's right, I forgot, no one ever cares about anything I do.

## MONDAY, APRIL 25

No school today, as it's Easter Monday. Not that I am looking forward to the torture of going back and seeing Wayne and Chloe holding hands.

Using my calculator, I've worked out that I've been awake for 30,717 days now. That's 737,208 hours without so much as a snooze. No wonder I'm getting tired.

# TUESDAY, APRIL 26

A ray of hope has entered my life! Chloe has dumped Wayne!

At lunchtime I provided her with a shoulder to cry on and found out the details. Apparently, Chloe dumped him for being a chauvinist.

If only I'd told Chloe that Wayne was sexist a couple of weeks ago, I could have avoided all that heartache.

According to Craig, Wayne's side of the story is that he dumped Chloe because she was clingy and needy.

The playground was buzzing with the news of the breakup today, and Brian said to me that I should grab Chloe on the rebound. Although I'm reluctant to take romantic advice from someone whose girlfriend looks like an extra from *The Lord of the Rings*, I think he might actually be on to something here.

### WEDNESDAY, APRIL 27
#### 7:00 a.m.

Today is the day I'm going to finally ask Chloe to be my girlfriend. I can't risk losing her again. This time I'm really going to do it.

#### 8:00 a.m.

Here I go! This is the last entry I shall write before finding true happiness.

## 10:00 a.m.

I waited outside the school gates for Chloe this morning, but when she arrived, she was with two girls from the popular gang, who were grilling her for gossip about the split. When will these vultures let her move on with her life?

## 11:00 a.m.

I said hello to Chloe after assembly, but she was late for math, so I didn't feel it was the right moment to declare my love. Timing is everything in the eternal dance of romance.

## 12:00 p.m.

I am now sitting in the library and waiting for Chloe to arrive. The girls from the popular gang never come here at lunchtime, so I'm certain she'll be alone this time. I'm so nervous, I've chewed off my entire fingernail and I'm currently waiting for it to grow back.

2:00 p.m.

I did it! I asked Chloe to be my girlfriend! And . . . she said she'd think about it! Brilliant! I think.

In truth, at first she seemed rather embarrassed by my request and said that she didn't want to jump into a relationship so soon after finishing with Wayne. I said I knew she was worried that Wayne would be upset to see her getting over him so quickly but that she should put her bad experience behind her and follow her heart. She seemed swayed by my argument, and told me she'd consider it and let me know her answer tomorrow.

12:00 p.m.

Tomorrow will either be the best or the worst day of my life. Ever since I got home, I've been lying in bed and wondering what Chloe will say. I wish I had vampire mind-reading skills like Dad's ex-girlfriend. At least that would get me out of the torture of waiting to discover my fate.

## THURSDAY, APRIL 28

Well, I have my answer now. Chloe has said that she likes me as a friend, but she doesn't want to go out with me. She was waiting outside the gates before school to drive these words into my heart. Needless to say, I went straight back to bed, and I've been here ever since.

To the annals of vampire lore, please add the following:

Throughout the history of our species, it's been thought that the most effective ways to destroy a vampire are to behead him or drive a stake through his heart. However, I have now discovered that telling a vampire that you like him as a friend but don't want to go out with him is far more effective.

That is all.

### FRIDAY, APRIL 29

I somehow managed to muster the strength to get out of bed today and trudge through my weary life.

As I was about to enter the school gates, I noticed that Chloe was once again waiting for me. I wondered what further punishment life could have in store for me. Perhaps she had decided that she didn't even like me as a friend anymore.

Chloe told me that she knew I'd been upset yesterday and wanted to explain herself. She said that she wasn't ready to have another boyfriend so soon after dumping Wayne and that she was afraid that I would also end up hating her if we split up, too, and that I'm the only proper friend she's made since she moved to this town.

She asked me if I was fine with all this, and I pretended that I was. But I think that there is hope once again.

## SATURDAY, APRIL 30

I spent today looking through Dad's books for

tips on how to deal with girls who only like you as a friend.

There was very little advice to be gleaned from them, which is hardly surprising when you consider that every other vampire in history was too beautiful to need advice on how to attract the opposite sex.

But I did find an interesting passage in a large book called *Thomas of Arundel's Vampire Almanac for the Year 1739, Being the Third After Leap Year, Wherein Is Contained Lessons for the Undead Regarding Industry, Temperance, and Frugality* (I'm guessing they weren't bothered about snappy book titles back then).

Inside, there was an account of a vampire from Devon who became infatuated with the only girl in his village who was immune to his powers of mesmerism. It says that in the end he got so impatient that he had to come right out and tell her he was a vampire to make her fall in love with him.

It said that all human women find vampires irresistible, but sometimes you need to reveal your supernatural status to make them fall for your charms. This sounds like a rather biased claim, but it's got to be worth a try.

## SUNDAY, MAY 1

I have no idea how to tell Chloe I'm a vampire. Obviously, I can't ask my parents for advice, as they'd go mad if they knew I was telling a human about us.

It's a bit of a risk, I suppose. For all I know, Chloe could be a vampire slayer posing as an ordinary schoolgirl with a secret undercover mission to destroy me and pick off my family one by one.

I must cease these paranoid thoughts! Everyone knows that vampire slayers don't even exist! They were just a scare story created by the vampire media hundreds of years ago to sell more pamphlets.

But it's possible she might be prejudiced against my kind. She might be opposed to blood-drinking on ethical grounds, like she is with foxhunting. I'm certainly not going to tell her about the hierarchy of victims outlined by the Vampire Council, as she is a liberal and would find it abhorrent.

## MONDAY, MAY 2

Wayne has accused me of stealing Chloe from him, even though I'm not actually going out with her yet. He told Craig to tell Paul to tell Si that he wants to fight me. Fearing that my reply would be deliberately misreported if I sent it back through these channels, I spoke to Wayne directly at lunchtime, letting him know that I'm not actually going out with Chloe and that I don't want to fight him.

I hope I've straightened it out, as I really

don't want to have to fight in front of everyone. Although Wayne couldn't do much to hurt
me, I know nothing about combat.

Dad once tried to teach me vampire martial
arts, but there's not much point in learning them
if you don't have supernatural strength and speed
in the first place. Whenever I tried to chop
blocks of wood with my hand, I kept breaking my
wrist, and we'd
have to wait
around for

it to heal. In the end, he got impatient and told me it would be better if I just phoned him if I was ever in danger.

# TUESDAY, MAY 3
## 5:00 p.m.

I tried to drop hints about my true nature to Chloe today, but she didn't pick up on them.

First, I asked her if she's ever wondered why she's never seen me eating, but she thought I was trying to tell her I was anorexic and said that I should tell the school nurse.

Next, I asked her if she's ever wondered why I'm so good at history. She pointed out that she beat me on the last test we had, so this clue didn't really work.

I then tried to change tack and told her that I don't sleep, but this only made her think

I was saying I had insomnia. She said that I should consider buying an herbal remedy or a book of relaxation techniques.

In the end I decided to go for broke and show her my high pain threshold and healing powers. I got the compasses out of my geometry set and was about to dig the point into my hand when she reached out to stop me.

She told me that she could see I was disturbed and that I mustn't harm myself just to prove it to her. She said that I should tell my doctor about the problems I'd revealed to her as they sounded serious.

Great. So now she thinks I'm a self-harming anorexic insomniac. That's hardly going to increase my sex appeal (except with Goth girls). Revealing my true nature to Chloe might prove more difficult than I thought.

12:00 p.m.

I've noticed that vampires in films make sly references to their nature when seducing human prey, so I've decided to slip these kinds of intriguing lines into conversation with Chloe. I've already come up with a few sophisticated ways to imply my nature:

"Music was so much better in the twenties."

"I don't like Dracula. It's not very realistic."

"Is that type O I can smell?"

"Your heartbeat sounds fast today."

"I apologize if I seem tetchy. I've been awake for the last 737,208 hours."

## WEDNESDAY, MAY 4

The subtle and sophisticated approach turned out to be a waste of time. I even took to raising my eyebrows before making the vampire references, but the penny didn't drop. I think I'm going to have to be more direct.

Stupid Mr. Jenkins is getting back on my case about PE lessons now that I've been off for three months. When he passed me in the hall at lunchtime, he said I was looking well. He was trying to catch me out, but I replied that my back still hurt.

That was a close shave. I didn't have my PE uniform with me, so I knew that Mr. Jenkins would make me do PE wearing something from the spare clothes box, which is full of torn, mismatched stuff. Just a small part of the humiliating revenge he has planned, no doubt.

I'm going to get Dad to say that I'm asthmatic and if Mr. Jenkins makes me do PE, I'll have an attack and the school will get sued. That should be enough to keep the fiend away from me.

## THURSDAY, MAY 5

Fate has handed a wonderful gift to me. There is a movie about vampires showing at the cinema. I shall invite Chloe to come and see it, and it will create the perfect excuse to reveal my true nature to her.

It's all so simple! Chloe will learn the truth and fall in love with me.

## FRIDAY, MAY 6

### 12:00 p.m.

So far, my plan is going without a hitch. Chloe has agreed to go to the movie with me. She has also agreed with my film choice, blissfully unaware that it shall mark her induction into the diabolical world of night.

Step into my trap, fragile prey.

### 4:00 p.m.

My brilliant plan has hit a big fat obstacle. Chloe told Brian from the Goths about our movie trip, and he has rudely invited himself along. Now John, as well as Brian's strange-looking girlfriend, are coming along too, which doesn't even make the right amount of people for a double date. Perhaps if I make sure I'm sitting next to Chloe on the end of the row, I can whisper the dark truth to her unheard by these surplus Goths. But I'm sure the smell of them alone will be enough to kill the mood.

## SATURDAY, MAY 7

Well, that was a waste of eight pounds plus bus fare. I failed to sit next to Chloe, reveal my true nature, or make her mine for the rest of eternity. And the film was rubbish!

Brian and John made a huge embarrassment of themselves on the way there by throwing spit balls at people from the bus window. If they're not mature enough to cope with traveling on their own, they shouldn't be allowed to. To make things worse, Brian's girlfriend was really egging them on.

Although I tried to position myself next to Chloe in the cinema, John barged in between us

and I ended up wedged between him and Brian's girlfriend, who bought a trough of popcorn and a vat of Coke. She kept alternating between slurping the Coke, munching the popcorn, and burping. From what I could hear between these disgusting noises (which wasn't much), the film was pretty appalling. It trotted out all the old vampirist crap about us sleeping in coffins, turning into bats, and crumbling into ash at the first sign of sunlight.

Still, Chloe said that she thought that the main vampire was "gorgeous," so my plan might well have worked if those other idiots hadn't lumbered along.

I managed to sit next to Chloe on the bus back, but my efforts to chat her up were sabotaged by Brian and John repeatedly pressing the bell to annoy the bus driver. In the end we were all thrown off and had to walk the rest of the way. Chloe was visibly irritated, and I was forced to abandon any further attempts at romance.

## SUNDAY, MAY 8
## 10:00 a.m.

Whenever I try to reveal my true nature to Chloe,

I find it hard to put it into words, so I've decided to set out the truth in a letter.

Darling Chloe,

I am writing to apologize for my behavior over the last few days. You might think I have been acting strangely since I declared my love for you. But the fact is, I have been trying to unveil a dark secret.

The truth is that I'm a vampire, and I am almost one hundred years old.

This might seem unbelievable or shocking to you. It might be a while before you are able to accept what I am saying. But if you consider the facts, you will come to accept it.

Have you ever wondered why I don't sleep? Why I don't eat? Why I feel no pain?

It is because I am one of the undead.

Do you feel drawn to me but overwhelmed by a mysterious sense of danger? Do I seem delicious but forbidden to you like a poisoned apple or some yogurt that's been accidentally left out of the fridge?

Am I right to suppose that there was a look of suspicion on your face that time in history when we watched a DVD called Life During Wartime? Did you understand that one of the teenagers in the black-and-white footage was actually me?

Yours in eternal admiration,

Nigel

P.S. If you didn't recognize me in the DVD, you can get it out of the library. Pause it after twelve minutes and thirty-five seconds and look in the top right corner of the screen.

P.P.S. Don't tell anyone about this.

P.P.P.S. Don't ask me to prove it by turning into a bat. All that stuff is made up.

### 1:00 p.m.

I have now mailed the letter. I am prepared for the consequences.

### 3:00 p.m.

I am beginning to regret mailing the letter. What if Chloe is repelled by my true nature? What if she shows it to her parents? What if my parents find out and abandon me for putting us all in danger?

### 6:00 p.m.

I am so stupid for writing our secrets down in a letter. What if the postman is a vampire slayer?

### 1:00 a.m.

Tonight I went out to retrieve the letter from the mailbox. At first I attempted to scoop it out

with a coat hanger, but that didn't work, so I
had to get my sister to use her vampire strength.
I had to beg her for ages before she agreed. I
ended up giving her thirty pounds from my savings
to buy a new Magical Princess Fashion Doll to

make her come down to the mailbox and rip it in
half so I could remove the letter.

So now I've wasted thirty pounds, pleaded

humiliatingly to my little sister, and damaged town council property, and all because I didn't have the guts to speak to Chloe directly.

No more excuses. Tomorrow I will tell Chloe the truth.

### MONDAY, MAY 9

Today went well for me. Or at least I think it did.

I stopped Chloe on the way back from school and told her I had something to reveal.

I tried again to tell her the truth, but my words kept coming out wrong. I said something about being a hundred, but she looked confused. I said something about how I don't have as much speed and strength as I should, but it didn't make things any clearer. Then I went off on a strange tangent about how I didn't really eat the candy she gave me in the library.

But as I was stumbling through this nonsense, she started to look at me differently. Her face turned from impatience and confusion to that hazy look I see on the faces of middle-aged women when Dad smiles at them. She reached toward me and the flow of blood in her wrists was so loud and fast that I couldn't hear what I was saying anymore.

My incoherent rambling was silenced when she pressed her finger against one of my teeth. It turns out that I'd been concentrating so hard on trying to reveal my true nature, I hadn't noticed that my fangs had extended and done the job for me.

Chloe ran her finger down one of them, as if to check they weren't from a joke shop.

And then, still in a dreamlike haze, she leaned forward and kissed me on the cheek!

She looked at me for a second with that gorgeous type-O blood filling her cheeks and then dashed off. And that was the last I saw of her.

Tonight I shall do nothing except relive that brief, sweet moment over and over again!

## TUESDAY, MAY 10

Yesterday I wasn't quite sure if the day had gone well. Well, I can confirm that today did, as Chloe has now agreed to be my girlfriend!

When I arrived at the school gates this morning, she was waiting for me again, and this time she asked me loads of questions about vampires. I told her about everything—my age, my family, my blood drinking. She found it hard to take in, but she was prepared to believe it now she'd seen my fangs.

Although she didn't admit it, I can tell she likes me more now that she knows I'm a vampire, just as the Almanac suggested. I just wish I'd revealed my supernatural nature sooner!

When I asked her if she'd be my girlfriend, she said yes! So now we are officially an item, although we've agreed to keep it secret from the rest of the school for the time being, as she doesn't want Wayne to get upset.

I don't care if he finds out! I don't care if he rams a stake through my heart! At least I would die happy!

## WEDNESDAY, MAY 11

I sat next to Chloe in history, and I spent the entire lesson drawing love hearts with her name in the middle and showing them to her. Then I drew a more realistic picture of a human heart, and I became intensely aware of the sound of blood spluttering through hers. I thought I might have gone too far with this drawing, so I kept it to myself.

I wonder when she'll let me drink her blood. Better take it one step at a time.

# THURSDAY, MAY 12

I sat next to Chloe in art this morning and we held hands all through the lesson. Let the school gossip; I'm not ashamed of our love.

An update on my ridiculous sibling: Tonight my sister tried to be controversial by putting a werewolf poster on her bedroom wall. She'd seen a film in which an army of vampires battle an army of werewolves, and she's decided that she wants to join "Team Werewolf" rather than "Team Vampire." Needless to say, we've all chosen to ignore her pathetic gesture of rebellion. I even told her that I fully approved of her decision to join Team Werewolf and offered to buy her a flea collar and a kennel to sleep in.

## FRIDAY, MAY 13

They say that Friday the Thirteenth is unlucky. Not for me, it wasn't. I had my first ever kiss today!!!

Chloe let me walk her back from school, and when we were almost at her house, she let me give her a kiss.

I then walked her up to her door and went home. And since then I've just been lying here in bed and feeling happy about the way things have turned out. The whole world seems different now.

## SATURDAY, MAY 14
## 6:00 p.m.

Happy birthday to me!!! Sweet one hundred today!!! And now that I finally have a girlfriend, I don't even feel too bad about reaching this milestone.

My human birthday is always a time for quiet contemplation rather than family celebration like my transformation day.

I spent today looking through the bags of old possessions I keep in my wardrobe: cards from the thirties, *Star Wars* figures from the seventies, and obsolete console games from the nineties. I even had a look at my photograph of the orphanage in London where I lived when I was human.

I was falling into a state of wistful reflection when another shrill and hateful dose of teen pop came blasting through the wall and snapped me out of it. Trust my sister to ruin this special day.

10:00 p.m.
I just texted Chloe good night. I considered phoning her, but we've only been going

out for four days and twelve hours, and I
didn't want to come across like an obsessive
stalker.*

12:00 p.m.
I have been going out with Chloe for four days
and fourteen hours now.

SUNDAY, MAY 15
6:00 p.m.
Today I harvested some human blood myself!
Bet you weren't expecting that. I went out for
a walk this afternoon, and I was crossing the
road when I heard a cry for help coming from
around a bend. I saw that a man had crashed
his van as he was turning a corner, and what a

---

*Apparently, it is an insult to call a human a stalker. This is a great
compliment in the vampire world.

stroke of luck—he was a messenger delivering blood to the hospital!

The man was dazed, so I called an ambulance on his phone. But I couldn't resist opening up the back of his van and making off with the blood. It was a bit naughty, but they must be aware of the temptation they're presenting when they write the word "Blood" on the front of their vehicles as if they were vampire ice-cream vans.

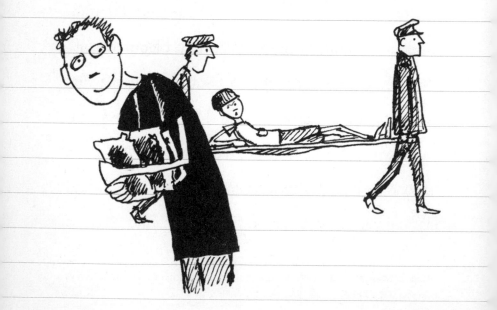

When I got home, Mum and Dad were very impressed that I'd managed to bring home some blood, even if it was just boring old type A+.

### 10:00 P.M.

I have been enjoying the blood I collected, but now I've started to feel slightly guilty. What if the person it was intended for is really ill? What if the messenger gets fired for losing it? What if the donor took the morning off work to give it?

I know I shouldn't worry about these things. Vampires are supposed to be able to glide around and glug human blood as they like, but I can't help but feel guilty about the people I affect.

Perhaps I am too sensitive to be undead.

### MONDAY, MAY 16

This morning I told Chloe how much I'd missed

225

her over the weekend. She said she'd missed me too and that she'd gotten a book about vampires out of the library to learn more about my culture. I told her that if she has any questions about the subject, she should ask my parents or me rather than reading some work of propaganda that claims we can all turn into bats.

She got very excited at the prospect of meeting Mum and Dad, and I immediately wished I hadn't mentioned it. I can understand why she's so curious to meet some other vampires, but I know that they'll find some way to embarrass me if I bring her round. Wearing strange old-fashioned clothes, playing the harpsichord, biting her. That kind of thing.

But I will discuss the matter with them as I promised. Anything for my darling Chloe.

Tonight I asked Mum and Dad if I could bring my girlfriend home to meet them, and I think it came as a shock. I don't know why it should—it's not like I'm a kid anymore.

Mum said that she'd always imagined I'd settle down with a nice vampire girl. How am I supposed to do that when there aren't any left?

Dad said that he was happy for me but that I should think very deeply about my decision to date someone from the mortal world.

Decision? Falling in love isn't a decision!

And think deeply? He hardly thought deeply when he was courting Mum in Paris two hundred years ago. According to him, he fed on her neck within moments of meeting her, transformed her after just a week, and they'd had their vampire wedding before the month was out. He's hardly in a position to lecture anyone about restraint.

11:00 p.m.
Dad has given me a pamphlet called *So You're Thinking of Loving a Mortal?* It looks ancient, and I'd be very surprised if it has anything relevant to say to a modern young vampire like me.

1:00 a.m.

Word has reached my sister that I have a girlfriend. Tonight she ran into my room and chanted
the following:

Nigel and Chloe sitting in a tree
K-I-S-S-I-N-G.
First comes love,
Then comes marriage,
Then comes Chloe with a baby carriage.

What my sister has failed to understand is
that when you're in a mature and adult relationship, it's not something you're ashamed of,
so this kind of teasing doesn't work. Also, given
that I'm a vampire, the only way we could ever
have a baby would be if I transformed a human
one and spent the rest of eternity feeding it

229

blood from a bottle every time it cried. And even the broodiest vampires have realized that's not a very clever idea.*

Though I was reluctant to sink to my sister's level, I soon realized that the only way I could get rid of her would be to accuse her of kissing a boy in her class called Kyle Brown. This had the desired effect of making her howl in shame and dash back to her room.

*The Vampire Council used to have a strict rule that you could only transform humans between the ages of seven and seventy. Anyone younger is likely to throw dangerous public tantrums, and anyone older just looks weird when they lift up huge rocks or run faster than cars.

## WEDNESDAY, MAY 18
### 6:00 p.m.

This morning both Craig and John the Goth asked if it was true that I was going out with Chloe. I said I had no comment on the matter, which they took as confirmation. I don't know why everyone is so surprised that I have a girlfriend. Perhaps when they're more mature, they'll understand love.

In the afternoon we had a biology lesson on the human digestive system, which was about how they eat food and turn it into poo. Humans are pretty disgusting when you think about it (not Chloe, she is fragrant and lovely, but all other humans are nasty).

It made me wonder about the digestive system of vampires. It's clearly different, because we don't need to go to the bathroom, but nobody has ever found out how it works. Perhaps I should donate my sister to science so they can find out.

10:00 p.m.

This evening I've been reading the pamphlet that Dad gave me. Needless to say, it's hopelessly outdated.

It's basically a work of propaganda produced by the Vampire Council that claims that vampires should fall in love with their own kind because loving mortals is too risky.

It says that vampires will be unable to control their desire to drink human blood, and this will cause problems. The mortal could die if too much blood is drained from them, or they could get infected with vampire blood and transform.

It says that many mortals will beg to be turned into vampires, but they won't understand what they're letting themselves in for. It's a really out-of-date leaflet because it

233

says there's a danger of vampire overpopulation if too many humans transform and every vampire will be fighting over the same scarce blood resources.

Overpopulation? According to Dad, we're the last vampires left. Surely extinction is a bigger danger than overpopulation.


1:00 a.m.

I told Dad that the leaflet hasn't put me off having a mortal girlfriend, and I think he's warming to the idea. I asked him if Chloe could come round for lunch on Sunday, and he agreed. He doesn't have any human friends, so I had to make it very clear to him that she is coming round to eat lunch rather than to *be* lunch. I think he understood.

## THURSDAY, MAY 19
### 1:00 p.m.

Wayne has found out that Chloe and I are an item, and apparently I'm going to fight him in the sports fields after school. I'm dreading it, not because I'm scared of Wayne, but because I hate it when everyone stares at me.

Chloe said she was disappointed with me for agreeing to the fight. I tried to explain to her that I hadn't agreed and had simply been informed by Craig that I would be taking part. For all I know, Wayne might have found out in exactly the same way.

Chloe then said that she's refusing to attend the childish fight that's being held in her honor and doesn't care who wins.

## 3:00 p.m.

Craig passed me a note in math that said that Wayne called me a goofy, pizza-faced jerk who's too scared to fight. Wayne would be lucky to escape with his life if that ever happened!

I think Craig is stirring it up.

## 7:00 p.m.

I've had my first ever fight now, and I have to say I found the whole thing very awkward. I dutifully made my way to the sports field this afternoon with an angry Wayne and an excited group of onlookers.

Once we were a good distance from the staff window, we dumped our bags on the ground and waited for everyone to cluster round.

Craig led the crowd in a rousing chant of "Have a fight! See who's best!" Wayne then gave me a shove, but I couldn't really be bothered pushing him back, so I just stood there. He seemed really angry, so I can only guess what Craig claimed I'd said about him.

I tried to defuse the situation by explaining to Wayne that I had made no attempt to date Chloe until she dumped him. Rather than calming him down, this made him even angrier, and he threw a series of clumsy slaps at me. Feeling no pain, and unaware of what the appropriate thing to do was, I suggested that we forget the whole silly business. I thought my attempts to make peace had succeeded. However, I saw a glint of true rage in his eyes and realized that he was preparing to throw a punch.

Unsure what else to do, I watched in curiosity as Wayne's fist hit me. I had a vague sense that I should pretend to be hurt when it made contact, but I felt too self-conscious to put on an act.

It didn't matter, anyway, as within a second of hitting me, Wayne was rolling around on the grass. It seems that when Wayne's hand crushed into my icy face, a bone in his index finger snapped.

Sensing that something serious had happened, most of the onlookers fled the scene. I offered to help Wayne, but he told me not to touch him, so I skulked off home.

As soon as I got inside the school gates, I was besieged by pupils asking me if it was true that I beat up Wayne so badly he had to go to the hospital. Even members of the tough gang were looking at me with admiration. Where were these fair-weather friends before?

I didn't really care what they thought. I was more concerned that Chloe would be angry with me for being violent.

I caught her in the corridor on the way to math, and she said that she'd heard about the fight. I was about to explain that I hadn't acted in aggression when she gave me a big kiss! And after she'd said she was a pacifist!

After one hundred years on this planet, I am still no closer to understanding girls.

7:00 p.m.

For a while today I was almost starting to feel proud of my victory. But by the afternoon word had reached the teachers that I beat up Wayne, and the principal took me into his office for a completely unfair telling off.

To be honest, getting told off by the principal isn't the harsh experience it once was, when you'd join a row of wrongdoers and wait for a whack of the cane.

But the punishment you get now is worse in its own way. We had to have a chat about my "aggressive tendencies," and I was forced to say that I now regretted my actions, which had made me less popular with my fellow students (the opposite is true), and that I'd learned that violence doesn't solve anything. The principal droned on about my "anger issues" for a while, but he eventually let me go.

## SATURDAY, MAY 21

I saw Jay and Baz from the tough gang riding a shopping cart around their estate this after-noon. They'd heard about the fight, and called me over to ask if I was a "hard case." I said I was and they told me to prove it by riding the cart down a flight of steps. I was happy to rise to their challenge, even though I couldn't really see the point.

The cart tipped over at the bottom of the stairs, and I flew out and broke my wrist. I put my hand in my jacket pocket to hide it while it healed, and Jay and Baz seemed impressed by my daring. I hope they don't ask me to become a full-time member of the tough gang, though. These sorts of hijinks would get very boring if you did them every day.

This evening I told Dad about the fight and Chloe's unexpected reaction, and he said that women always love it when men fight over them, even though they pretend they don't. Dad's views about women are often very outdated, but I think he might be on to something this time.

I phoned Chloe tonight, and she said she's looking forward to coming round to my house tomorrow. I warned her not to crack any jokes about turning into bats or sleeping in coffins, as these are offensive to my people.

## SUNDAY, MAY 22

Chloe came round today. I was worried that the visit might feel awkward, but I forgot about the mesmeric effect that my parents have on humans. Far from sitting in uncomfortable silence, Chloe instantly fell under their spell.

As they made small talk with Chloe, I could see her glancing from Dad to Mum, entranced by them. She didn't even mind when my sister barged rudely in for a stare.

After about an hour of chatting, we moved into the dining room and I was concerned to see that Mum and Dad had set places for all of us at the table. Mum microwaved a meal of chicken and vegetables for Chloe, and spooned it out onto the plate as if it were dog food.

Chloe thanked her and started eating. However, the atmosphere turned less cozy when Mum served glasses of blood for the rest of us. I think my parents just wanted to join in with Sunday lunch so Chloe wouldn't have to eat on her own, but it's easy to forget how disconcerting the sight of blood-drinking can be to a non-vampire. Especially if you let it run all down your chin like my messy sister did!

Chloe lost her appetite and left the rest of her food. She kept on smiling politely, but you could tell she felt uncomfortable, and she left shortly afterward. This is what happens with humans. They find the idea of vampires glamorous and romantic but the reality less pleasant.

I can only hope that my parents' rash behavior hasn't turned her against me.

## MONDAY, MAY 23

This morning I asked Chloe if seeing us drink blood had put her off me. She said that she'd found it a little disturbing, but she understood it was part of our culture. She is so tolerant and understanding!

I think she's right. I don't see any reason why I should be ashamed of my need to drink blood. It might look unpleasant, but so do hundreds of things that humans do all the time, like wearing tight swimming trunks or combing their hair all the way across their heads when they go bald.

Of course, some would say that feeding on humans is unethical because it can weaken or kill them, but I don't think it's as bad as a lot of the things humans do. I bet if you added together all the injuries and deaths that have ever been caused by vampires, they wouldn't approach the damage mankind inflicts upon itself in the average war.

One of the best things about having a girl-friend is that it helps you to accept yourself and find confidence. For the first time in my life I no longer feel ashamed of being a vampire.

246

# TUESDAY, MAY 24
## 9:00 a.m.

I finally feel ready to share my poetry with Chloe. I have written a new one, which I intend to show her today. I put lots of care into it and even used a thesaurus, which lists lots of words that mean the same thing, so you can write longer poems.

## BLOOD SYMPHONY

As you sleep, I watch

The moonlight on your neck

And listen to your blood.

It is a harmony of hemoglobin.

A symphony of sanguine fluid.

A prelude of plasma.

A concerto of claret.

A guitar solo of gore.

Play on, sweet music.

3:00 p.m.

I gave Chloe a copy of the poem today, and she said it was very good. She covered up her neck when she read it, though, so perhaps some of the imagery was a little too explicit.

## WEDNESDAY, MAY 25

Dad was out tonight, so I went to his study to look for books on vampire-human relationships. The only ones I could find were written by vampire supremacists who regarded humans as little more than walking snacks, so they weren't much use. One of Dad's bookmarks fell out, and when I picked it up, it turned out to be a letter from his ex-girlfriend, the psychic vampire.

The letter was giving him all sorts of grief about things he hadn't done yet, and I could understand why she would have been so difficult to live with. But there was one part of the letter that I found intriguing. She mentioned some trouble that Dad would encounter this year! It wasn't very specific. I wonder if she was referring to the time in January when he drank the blood with a high level of alcohol in it and got ill.

I was going to ask Dad about it, but I thought he might be angry with me for going through his stuff, so I decided not to say anything. Plus, if she was such a good psychic, she'd have been able to predict that she was going to get beheaded in the great vampire purge of 1878, so I doubt it's anything to worry about.

## THURSDAY, MAY 26

Someone farted in assembly today, and everyone seemed to think it was the funniest thing that had ever happened. I didn't share their opinion. Perhaps it's because I don't have a human digestive system and can't pass wind myself that I don't find this bodily function especially funny. Or maybe I just have a more sophisticated sense of humor (I once laughed at an Oscar Wilde play).

Afterward Chloe noted that we were the only two people in the hall who didn't laugh, and that includes Mr. Jones, who was taking assembly. She said that we are much more mature than everyone else in our school.

I suppose I ought to be mature given that I'm one hundred years old. But I'll take compliments where I can get them, especially from my darling girlfriend!

## FRIDAY, MAY 27

Chloe has invited me to her house for a meal on Sunday. Although I'm pleased that she's ready to take our relationship up to this level, I'm not sure how I'm going to get through it. Chloe has told her parents I'm allergic to garlic, but she needs to understand that my situation is more complicated than this. She thinks I can just swallow the food to be polite, but it doesn't work like that. Anything I try to force down will come right back up again. Which is hardly a good first impression to make.

I suppose I could pretend to have an upset

stomach, but they'll wonder why I came round at all if I'm ill.

Perhaps if I sit next to the radiator, I can slip the food down there discreetly. But this could cause an unpleasant stench, especially if they make tuna bake or macaroni and cheese.

## SATURDAY, MAY 28

I think I've come up with a good solution to the food problem. I've taken one of my dad's old jackets and sewn a couple of plastic bags inside the sleeves. Using sleight of hand, I'll pretend to put the food in my mouth while letting it fall into the bags. I've been practicing, and I reckon I can do it quickly enough to avoid suspicion.

My food jacket was a success, at first.

I called round at Chloe's house on time, and waited to be invited inside by her parents.* I shook hands with them, complimenting them on their choice of furniture to distract from my cold temperature.

We sat down for lunch and Chloe's dad poured me a glass of fresh orange juice, which I pretended to sip. Chloe's mum then served the meal she had prepared, which was roast beef, boiled potatoes, and carrots. I felt sorry for her when I saw the pride with which she dished it out. If only she'd left my cut of beef out of

---

*I waited out of politeness, although I'm also rather superstitious about entering human residences. According to folklore, vampires experience intolerable pain if they enter a home without first being asked in.

As ever, the myth doesn't really stand up to scrutiny. Does everyone who lives there have to invite you in? Do you need permission from the landlord if they're renting? Nonetheless, I don't feel it's worth the risk. "Intolerable pain" doesn't sound much fun to me.

the oven I could at least have sucked the blood out of it.

I congratulated Chloe's mum on her cooking as I discreetly tucked it up my sleeves. When I had cleared my plate, I excused myself, locked myself in the bathroom, and flushed the food down the toilet. The carrots kept floating up again, and it took me five flushes to get rid of it all.

I took my place again at the table downstairs, but just when I was beginning to think I was out of the woods, Chloe's mum produced an enormous sponge pudding and jug of custard. Despite my protestation that I was full, she insisted on doling out a huge portion. I managed to get it into the plastic bags in my sleeves, but they got so full that I had to keep my arms held up at my sides to avoid custard seepage.

I just about managed to get away with it until it was time to leave and Chloe's dad held out his hand for me to shake. Not wanting to let the custard slide onto his hand, I was left with no choice but to shout, "High five!" He looked rather surprised but held his hands up and I slapped my palms against his.

As soon as I was out of sight, I poured the foul custard down the drain.

# MONDAY, MAY 30

The school holidays started again today, and for once they were welcome, as I got to spend some quality time with Chloe away from the attention of the school gossipers.

This morning we went down to the mall. Chloe said that people who spend their lives looking around shops are shallow and materialistic, so we bought some serious newspapers and went for a coffee. Chloe had a frappuccino, and I got a cup of ice and poured some blood into it from my flask. I felt like a normal well-adjusted teenager, sipping a frappuccino in a coffee franchise with my girlfriend. Admittedly, it was a human blood frappuccino, but apart from that it was completely normal and well-adjusted.

I couldn't find much in the serious newspaper

that interested me. There was a page of computer game reviews and a couple of comics, but that was about it. Chloe read all the news stories in her paper, though, even the ones about other countries! She is so mature!

## TUESDAY, MAY 31

I went out for a romantic walk in the countryside with Chloe today. It was nice to walk at human pace instead of trying to keep up with my family.

Chloe said I should take my jacket off because it was hot, but I said I didn't want to in case I got a rash. She said that I shouldn't be ashamed of my rashes as they are part of who I am as a vampire. Let's hope she's this understanding about vampire culture when I ask to drink her blood!

I tied my jacket against my waist and felt a wonderful sense of abandon as I waved my bare arms around. When I got home, Mum saw my red arms and went mad because I had forgotten to put sunblock on. I told her I was in love and had no time for such trivial concerns.

## WEDNESDAY, JUNE 1

Chloe is going to see her aunt tomorrow. When I tried to persuade her to stay here with me, she said that she couldn't neglect her family duties, but because of the request I made in my poem, she's decided to let me sit in the tree outside her bedroom window and watch her sleep.

I can't do many of the romantic things that vampires do for human women, like carrying them to Paris for the weekend, but I'm sure I can manage to sit in a tree for a few hours. I have arranged to be in the tree at half past twelve tonight, after her parents have fallen asleep, at which point Chloe will open her bedroom curtain.

Spoiled brat update: My sister has announced that she wants to learn to ride a pony. What a ridiculous idea! Imagine the fuss all the animals would make if she strolled into a horse riding center. I told her about my experience in the zoo, but she took no notice.

Even if the ponies were stupid enough to let my sister near them, how long would she be able to resist sticking her teeth into one of their veiny necks?

When will my sister accept that she's not the princess of a magical rainbow kingdom, but a ruthless and bloodthirsty killer like the rest of us?

Spoiled brat newsflash: My parents told my sister she isn't allowed pony lessons. Anyone would think they were rational, fair, and sen-sible. I don't know why they're acting so out of character.

# THURSDAY, JUNE 2

Chloe has gone to visit her aunt, and I'm resting at home in bed, feeling a little sore after my night in the tree.

I arrived at half past twelve as agreed, but I couldn't get up the tree at first. I ended up having to use the ladder from the back of their shed, which hardly enhanced the atmosphere of supernatural romance.

When Chloe saw me in the tree, she waved and then went to bed. It took her a while to go to sleep, because every time she opened her eyes to check and I was still there, this made me laugh, and then she laughed, too.

When she did get to sleep, I have to confess that I found the experience pretty dull. I stared at her and thought about my undying love for an hour or so, but then my mind began to wander. I was tempted to nip down to the all-night convenience store and buy a magazine, but I was worried that she might wake up and question the seriousness of my feelings.

Around 3:00 a.m., I took my phone out of my pocket and played Snake until the batteries died. Chloe started snoring at around 4:00 a.m., and it was so loud, I could hear it through the glass. She woke up at 6:30 a.m., waved good-bye through her window, and then I left.

It was good to do some proper romantic vampire stuff, but I think I'll bring a crossword next time.

FRIDAY, JUNE 3
12:00 p.m.

I can't begin to express the heartache I feel upon being separated from my true love. This is probably how Sebastian of Lyon felt when his lover was imprisoned in the Bastille for twenty years. Except he didn't have the option to send texts like I do.

1:00 a.m.

I went out for a walk in the graveyard again tonight to take my mind off my heartache, and guess who I saw there?

It was Dad, lurking behind one of the graves!

263

Resisting the urge to let him know I'd caught him red-handed, I stayed back a good distance and observed him. I couldn't believe that he'd denied responsibility for the attacks on the local townspeople, and yet here he was, hanging around the graveyard at midnight, waiting for the next victim to snack on. How dare he put my happiness at risk for the sake of his own greed?

In the far distance I could see a woman enter the graveyard alone. Spotting his chance, Dad swooped. I tried to run after him and let him know he was caught, but I was unable to match his vampire speed and could only watch from a distance as he sated his foul appetite on the innocent.

Eventually I caught up with him and was just about to take him to task when I realized that the woman he was attacking wasn't a passing human at all, but Mum! And the worst thing is that they were kissing! It was so disgusting.

Looking very sheepish and embarrassed, they explained to me that it was the anniversary of the time they first met, and they were celebrating by re-creating it.

I told them that I didn't want to know anything about their sordid activities, but they should at least tell me if they're going out at night, as my sister has been left at home on her own thanks to their irresponsible behavior. What if a burglar came in?

To be fair, the burglar would be in more danger than my sister, but I was enjoying the moral high ground too much to concern myself with such minor points.

## SATURDAY, JUNE 4

I have written a poem to help me cope while Chloe is away. I considered sending it to her, but I'm worried she might find it too graphic. Plus, it's slightly too long to fit on a text. When the time comes for my work to be published, Chloe cannot be shielded from the intensity of my feelings, but until then I'll keep them secret.

# I WAIT IN ETERNAL PAIN

With your neck so long and blood so sweet

Life without you is incomplete

How I long to drink from your vein

Instead I wait in eternal pain


## SUNDAY, JUNE 5

Chloe's dad will be driving her back home now. I hope he's a safer driver than my dad and that my love isn't stolen away from me by a fatal crash, dooming me to eternal grief. That would be just typical.

In a few hours' time, we shall be reunited. Come swiftly, precious hour!


## MONDAY, JUNE 6

I went back to school today and was reunited with my true love. I told her that the last four days had been the longest of my life, although from the sound of it, they would have felt even longer if I'd gone to her aunt's with her.

Wayne is going out with Sally Mulligan now. I think he's only doing it to get revenge on Chloe and me, because at the bus stop after school he kept his arm around Sally and laughed loudly whenever she said anything; then he'd look over at us to see if we noticed. Neither of us particularly cared. We are in a proper, adult relationship now and have no need to concern ourselves with the trivial lives of our immature classmates.

Plus, I know I'm better-looking than him because Chloe said so.

## TUESDAY, JUNE 7

Today was so sunny that Chloe let me give her a hug. Because I'm so cold, Chloe is usually reluctant to hug me unless she's wearing a sweater. But today she said she found my temperature soothing.

I'd better enjoy it while I can, because she's not going to want my freezing body anywhere near her when winter comes around again.

## WEDNESDAY, JUNE 8

A weird thing happened at lunchtime today. Chloe was looking at me in the library when a dreamy and distant look came into her eyes. I asked her if she was all right, but she just kept staring at me with strange contentment.

After a couple of minutes I alerted the librarian, who took Chloe to the school nurse. She needed to lie down but was soon feeling fine again. The nurse interrogated her for a further twenty minutes about whether she'd taken any alcohol or drugs, and then she let her go. She was right as rain again in time for business studies.

When I walked Chloe home later, she still seemed fine. I asked her about her experience at lunchtime, and she said that the room went swirly, she could hear a distant piano and smell rose petals, and she felt very safe and relaxed. The more I think about it, the more Chloe seems to have been showing the effects of vampire hypnosis.

But I don't have the vampire power of mesmerism, so I've no idea how that could have
happened. How strange.

## THURSDAY, JUNE 9

We sneaked into the music room at lunchtime so
I could show Chloe my piano skills. I started with
simple pieces like "Chopsticks" and "The Camptown
Races," so she would be more impressed by
what followed, then launched into Beethoven's
*Moonlight* sonata. Chloe was overjoyed at my
skills, but I didn't want to look directly at her
in case I mesmerized her again and the nurse
became convinced she was a drug addict.

I broke off and explained to Chloe that during eight and a half decades with no sleep, you
get a lot of time to hone your skills. She asked
what else I'd developed a talent for, but the

only things I could think of were Connect Four and Tetris, so I turned back to the piano and continued playing.

## FRIDAY, JUNE 10

Craig played an explicit rap song on his phone in math today. The rapper was being rude about a rival, and everyone was really impressed with all the swearing, but I didn't think it was a big deal.

It's nothing new, anyway. Dad told me that a vampire called Ludovico of Sienna once published an epic poem about how a love rival was igno-rant, loathsome, and tedious. He was found dead with a wooden stake through his heart two weeks later in what was thought to be a ride-by staking.

Mum and Dad are going down to London again tomorrow, so I'm going to invite Chloe round and play the piano for her. I might even light one of Mum's ancient candelabras and put on one of Dad's capes. I used to think all that stuff was really corny, but the more I vamp it up, the more Chloe seems to like me, so I'm happy to go along with it all now.

I don't mind playing up to stereotypes if it keeps her happy!

## SATURDAY, JUNE 11

Chloe came round at six this evening and said that she'd promised her parents she'd be back before nine. That didn't give me much time to establish the melodramatic mood.

I had a quick check to make sure nobody was walking past and then opened the door to show her my suit and cape. She stifled a laugh when she saw me, but I could tell she thought it was really sexy.

I have to say, I don't quite understand why capes were so popular with vampires. I think it had something to do with shielding your skin from the sun, but I found it highly impractical. It kept swishing out behind me and knocking things off tables. Running around a candle-strewn castle with one of these things on sounds like a blatant fire hazard to me.

When Chloe was inside, I sat at the piano and launched into Chopin's Funeral March (no vampire cliché is too cheesy when romance is on the cards).

Then I sat next to her and was just about to
roll out some line about how I've searched through
the endless fog of time for her when my annoying
sister walked in and asked us what we were doing.

I told her that we were having a private
conversation, but she failed to take the hint
and plonked herself down on an armchair. Chloe
politely chatted with her while I threw in a

series of unsubtle suggestions about how she probably had something else to do, all of which went right over her dense little head.

In the end all I got was a kiss on the cheek, which isn't much when you consider all the effort I put in.

## SUNDAY, JUNE 12

Chloe has gone to church this morning, and there was no question of me tagging along. All those crucifixes would give me a splitting headache, and the rest of the day would be a write-off.

So now I've been on the PlayStation for seven hours straight. Craig once told me that computer games aren't as exciting once you get a girlfriend. I didn't believe him, but now I think it might actually be true.

Perhaps I'm becoming mature.

Chloe has several nicknames for me now because that's what happens in serious relationships. She calls me Fangy, Mr. Freeze, and Nige of the Living Dead. I thought these lacked gravitas, so I've suggested that she call me Nightwalker instead. So far my suggestion has not been taken on board.

I had to see the guidance counselor today. Over the years I've developed a strategy of pretending I want to work in a sector that I know they've got a flyer on, like health care or retail, so I can make the meeting as short as possible. Unfortunately, this particular guidance counselor insisted on grilling me about my interests. I played along, even though it doesn't matter what I want to do in the future, because I'll be a school student until society breaks down so much that schools no longer exist.

In the end she gave me a leaflet about IT and I tossed it at the first opportunity. After her meeting, Chloe decided she wanted to help disadvantaged children in Africa. I admired her selflessness, but I tried to steer her away from the plan because Africa would be too hot for me.

## TUESDAY, JUNE 14

I was happily drinking some blood when Dad came into my room looking awkward. He sat down on the edge of the bed and explained that as I had a human girlfriend now, it was time that we had a talk about safe feeding. I told him that I didn't have any plans to feed on Chloe, but that didn't stop him from going on about how you have to avoid mixing blood with humans in case they transform into vampires.

278

We then sat in uncomfortable silence for a couple of minutes until he handed me another one of his old-fashioned pamphlets. I think if it were possible for vampires to blush, we'd have both been bright red!

## WEDNESDAY, JUNE 15

Chloe was engrossed in her homework this lunchtime, so I went out behind the gym to hang around with the Goths instead.

I shouldn't have bothered. They kept asking if my girlfriend was busy and saying that they thought they weren't worthy of my attention anymore. It was really immature and motivated by jealousy.

I did my best to ignore it, but I started to get riled when John said in a really sarcastic voice that I should go and check that my "princess" was all right.

So I have officially broken friends with the Goths now. Who needs friends when you have a girlfriend, anyway?

## THURSDAY, JUNE 16

The leaflet Dad has given me is called *Feeding on Humans Without Bleeding on Humans*. Although it had a serious message, I couldn't help laughing at the diagrams because they were so out of date. All the men were wearing huge velvet capes and the women were wearing gowns and corsets.

Nonetheless, I made an effort to take in all the safety advice in the leaflet. I just hope I can remember it if my hunger ever gets the better of me.

## FRIDAY, JUNE 17

Tomorrow I'm calling round at Chloe's house, and then we're going out for a romantic walk in the park. Apparently it's going to be a hot day, so I'm putting on extra sunblock. Should be good.

## SATURDAY, JUNE 18
### 9:00 a.m.

A strange start to the morning. Chloe has dropped a note through our mail slot instructing me to meet her at the school gates rather than her house. It's definitely her writing, and nobody else knows she calls me Fangy, but I find it odd that she chose to write a note rather than ring the doorbell and tell me. It's not like she would have been waking anyone up.

The school isn't on the way to the park, so I think she has a surprise trip planned. I'm off to meet her now, though I'm a bit wary about going near school on weekends. There was an incident last October when a group of ex-students broke in on a Saturday and draped toilet paper around the corridors. I wouldn't like to be falsely associated with a weekend toilet paper attack if it happens again. I had enough trouble after my "fight" with Wayne.

6:00 p.m.
Well, that was a stressful day, to say the least. When I got to the gates of the school, I found

another note in Chloe's handwriting telling me to go to the gym. I had no idea what she would be doing in there on a Saturday. The only thing I could think of was that she might be helping with the preparations for the summer fair.

I saw that the fire doors to the gym were open, so I went in. As soon as I got inside, I felt like I was surrounded by bright flashing lights while the sound of metal scraping on metal was blasted directly into my brain. I fell down to the floor with my hands on my head trying to work out what was happening and why Chloe thought that this would be a pleasant way for me to spend my Saturday.

The scene in front of me gradually came into focus, and I could see a barrier of bookshelves filled with crucifixes stretching across the width of the gym. All around me, the floor was covered in pungent cloves of garlic.

My first instinct was to run away, but as I forced myself to ignore the pounding in my head, it dawned on me that someone must know I'm a vampire and I must be in trouble.

Was this an elaborate revenge planned by Wayne? Was it the Goths' idea of a practical joke? Could it really be true that Chloe was a vampire slayer, as I had once speculated?

This last possibility was ruled out when I saw my darling girlfriend in a gap between two of the bookcases, tied to a chair and with a gag in her mouth. A figure was lurking behind her, and through the haze of my migraine I saw that it was Mr. Jenkins, the PE teacher!

I told him I was sorry I had lied about having a bad back, but kidnapping my girlfriend and

torturing me was surely an excessive punishment.

He asked me if I was really stupid or just pretending, which I thought was a bit rich coming from a PE teacher. He then bent down toward Chloe and took a good sniff of her neck. I wanted to get up and stop him, but I was still too weak from all the garlic and crucifixes.

Mr. Jenkins looked at me and said that he loved the smell of type O. Then he smiled, exposing two elongated fangs! I couldn't believe it! My stupid PE teacher was one of us!

My head was spinning so much that it took a while for everything to fall into place, but at last I realized that it must have been Mr. Jenkins who was responsible for the rogue vampire attacks in town, and not my parents after all. For a minute I almost felt relieved, until I looked up again and saw his ugly face smirking at me.

Mr. Jenkins told me that he knew all about my family and that if I didn't find a way to bring my dad to the gym by nightfall, he would drain Chloe's veins so much that she'd never wake up again. Then he stooped down and pressed his fangs right up to her jugular!

I managed to extract a promise out of him that he would release Chloe if I brought Dad in. So I crawled out of the gym and stumbled back home, where I'm writing this and waiting for Dad to get back from his Saturday hike. As usual, he's not answering his phone.

I wish my stupid dad would hurry up and get here. He is putting my happiness at risk!

## 12:00 a.m.

Okay, I admit that if I'd thought about it, I would have realized that I was leading Dad into danger. But it's hard to think rationally when your PE teacher has just taken the love of your life captive.

So when Dad got home, I told him he had to come to the school gym as I'd be performing in a surprise talent show that evening. It wasn't a very good lie, and he was hardly falling over himself to get there, but I thought it was an invitation he couldn't really turn down.

I know it was wrong of me to deceive Dad, but I'd just found out that he'd been lying to me my whole life about us being the last remaining vampires. If even the PE teacher at my school was a vampire, then how many others were still around? Perhaps he didn't want to alarm me. Perhaps he was frightened that I'd run off and join another coven. Either way, he should have told me the truth.

I ushered Dad through the door of the gym, telling him that the show was about to begin. The garlic and crucifixes floored us both when we got inside. I was prepared for it this time, but it was still really painful. I thought it might

be easier for Dad to ignore the vampire repel-
lents, but he seemed to be in just as much agony
as me. By the time I managed to ignore my
headache enough to see again, Dad was squint-
ing at the gap between the bookshelves.

I heard him ask if it was "Vaclav" he could
see. I was about to tell him that it was just
my stupid PE teacher who was causing all the
trouble when Mr. Jenkins replied, "Of course
it is. You didn't think you could hide from me
forever, did you?"

The weird thing was, my dad apologized to
Mr. Jenkins. I would have expected him to be
angry rather than sorry. Mr. Jenkins said there
was no way he could be expected to show mercy
when he had been shown none himself.

Mr. Jenkins was good to his promise and
released Chloe. She ran toward me and helped

me to my feet. She was about to offer my dad a hand too, when Mr. Jenkins pulled out a Super Soaker water gun from behind one of the bookshelves. He told us that it was loaded with holy water and he'd cover my dad with it if we tried to rescue him. We were forced to

leave Dad and Mr. Jenkins alone in the gym as we made our escape.

Chloe helped me stagger out of the fire exit and across the playground. As I walked away from the gym and my headache faded, I began to think more clearly. We paused at the railings on the edge of the playground, and I stopped feeling frightened and started feeling angry. I thought about how Mr. Jenkins had manipulated me to trap Dad and how long he must have been planning his revenge. But the thing that really tipped me over the edge was remembering how he'd threatened to drink Chloe's blood. My dear, sweet Chloe! The one mortal who understands and accepts me! How dare that vile fiend threaten her?

A look of alarm on Chloe's face snapped me out of my rage. I followed her gaze and saw that I'd somehow managed to bend back the iron railings I was holding on to. I tried bending the railing next to it, and it gave like it was made of tinfoil. I bent another railing and then another. I could now feel a strength and power I had never known before flowing through my body.

I ran back to the gym in a matter of seconds and looked up at the high windows. I became aware that I was about to jump up high into the air and crash through one of them. Usually I would have been worried about doing this in case I landed in a funny way or got some glass in my eye, but I didn't consider any of this. I wasn't thinking rationally at all, to be honest. I was moving so fast by this point that I'm finding it hard to remember exactly what was going through my mind.

I know I jumped through the window and landed
on the floor beside Mr. Jenkins. Now I was on
the other side of the bookshelves, at a safe
distance from the garlic and crucifixes and in a
good position to attack. Mr. Jenkins was ranting

at my dad, but he turned his attention to me as I charged forward.

I think Mr. Jenkins was surprised at my new-found speed and strength, especially as I could hardly manage a push-up last time I'd been in one of his PE lessons. He tried attacking me with a flying kick, but I blocked it and forced him into a corner. He tried to punch me, but I caught his hand and pinned him against the wall. I would have said, "How's this for a push-up?" But I didn't think of it at the time.

Mr. Jenkins wriggled free and jumped up to the top of the climbing bars on the gym wall. I leaped after him and ripped off one of the rungs to create a makeshift wooden stake. I tried desperately to ram it into his heart while he batted it away in terror.

I was getting the better of the struggle

when I heard Dad calling from below. He said that we were vampires, and this was not how vampires do things.

He then started reeling off some ancient mumbo jumbo I couldn't follow, but it must have meant something to Mr. Jenkins, because he climbed down and solemnly nodded his head. I did the same. It was only as we were walking Chloe home that Dad revealed I'd agreed to fight a duel with Mr. Jenkins under the ancient rules of the Vampire Council.

## SUNDAY, JUNE 19

In my anger last night, I forgot that killing Mr. Jenkins would have meant permanent exclusion from vampire society. I would have had to leave Mum and Dad's house. And you can bet my sister would have moved straight into my room.

She's always been jealous of me for having the biggest bedroom.

I am to fight the duel against Mr. Jenkins at midnight next Saturday in the park. Neither of us will die, but one of us will eventually surrender and go into exile for a hundred years under terms dictated by the winner. I don't know exactly what Mr. Jenkins has planned for me, but I bet it will involve push-ups.

If I win, I've decided to banish Mr. Jenkins to a small town in Kenya called Nanyuki, because I saw on a map that it's right over the equator, so I'm guessing it gets loads of sunlight. Even if he worms his way into another PE teaching job, the sun will prevent him from torturing the students too much.

The annoying thing is that Mr. Jenkins was in the middle of challenging my dad to a duel when

I jumped in through the window, but because I attempted to kill him, I now have to take part in the duel instead. To be honest, I wish I'd left them to it.

### MONDAY, JUNE 20
### 9:00 a.m.

Dad has phoned school to say I'll be off sick this week as it's forbidden for me to see Mr. Jenkins before the duel. I doubt he'll turn up at school, either, as he'll be too busy honing his vampire kung fu. I'm not going to waste my time worrying what he's up to, though. I need to focus on my own preparation.

This afternoon I went to the park to test my vampire speed,

and I ended up circling the whole thing in a matter of seconds!

It's funny to think that I was so convinced I didn't have vampire powers, while they were in me all along, waiting to be set off. Perhaps the emergency situation I found myself in on Saturday forced me to unleash them. Or perhaps being in love has given me the confidence to access powers I've always had. I'd write a poem about it if I weren't so busy.


## 7:00 p.m.

Dad is supposed to be teaching me vampire martial arts today, but he's still angry with me for luring him to the school gym and putting him at the mercy of Mr. Jenkins.

I've said sorry. He needs to get over it.

Anyway, I should be annoyed with him! He

said we were the last four vampires on earth! Now it turns out there are hundreds of us still around, and some of them, like Mr. Jenkins, have long-standing vendettas against Dad for transforming them. He says it only happened when he was young and reckless, and he doesn't see why they still want revenge on him now that he's settled down with a family.

I'm not allowed to tell my sister any of this, as Dad says she'll be happier not knowing, just as I would have been. The difference, though, is that I'm mature enough to cope with the truth. And rather than wasting my time accusing my parents of attacking the local townspeople, I could have been searching for the real culprit.

I have no doubt that I'd have used my powers of deduction to identify Mr. Jenkins as the true perpetrator, and this whole unpleasant situation would have been avoided.

## TUESDAY, JUNE 21
3:00 p.m.

I went out to the countryside this morning to try and get some control over my vampire speed and strength. I think I'm getting there. All I have to do is stand at the bottom of a cliff and focus on the energy building up inside me, and a few seconds later I find I've jumped right to the top.

It feels amazing to finally access my powers after so many years of believing I didn't have them. I was having a great time splashing through streams, leaping up hills, and uprooting trees, but I had to remind myself that I was here to train, not to mess around. It's brilliant to finally have these abilities, but they won't be much use if Mr.

Jenkins commands me to spend

the next one hundred years

on a desert island living

off stinky fish

blood.

7:00 p.m.

Chloe came round after school today. She's been

grounded for staying out late on Saturday and has

chosen to take the punishment rather than reveal

anything about us. I am deeply moved by her loyalty.

I ran down the street in just four seconds to

impress her, but she told me I should preserve my

energy for the duel. She said that she's very

worried about it, especially as she won't even

be allowed out to watch it. I told her I'd text

her afterward and that even if I was banished to somewhere horrible, she was welcome to join me. I don't think I sold that idea very well, because she changed the subject.

She said she felt foolish for going into the school on Saturday with Mr. Jenkins, but he told her that someone had spray-painted graffiti all over the gym and her sense of duty as a class officer took over from her common sense.

She gave me a quick kiss and rushed off home. I would have liked her to stay longer, but in my current vampirey mood I didn't trust myself to hold back from sinking my fangs into her neck, so it was probably for the best.

## WEDNESDAY, JUNE 22

My sister couldn't believe it when I offered to play soccer with her today. Mum and Dad hadn't told her that I'd finally gotten my vampire powers, and you could tell she was looking forward to dishing out another humiliating defeat.

She took her penalties first, and I let her score them all, as usual. But when she went in to goal, I blasted the ball at her with such force that it carried her through the back of the net and into the fence at the bottom of the garden. She tried to kick the ball back at my face, but I batted it away with ease. She then charged toward me at top speed and couldn't believe it when I ducked out of the way. She ended up chasing me around the garden at such a pace that we destroyed the lawn and Mum sent both of us to our rooms.

My sister's in a foul mood now that she's worked out I've gotten my speed and strength. Anyone would think she'd be pleased for me. She's probably worried that she might stop being the center of attention for once in her spoiled life.

Tonight I have been trying to learn vampire kung fu from one of Dad's crusty old manuals, but it's very difficult to hold on to a book when you're performing a forty-foot back flip. I hope he stops fuming and agrees to teach me soon.

## THURSDAY, JUNE 23

Dad has finally given in and agreed to train me. About time, too. Anyone would think he wanted me to go into exile.

We drove to a field in the remote country-side to ensure that we couldn't be seen, and Dad demonstrated the basic moves of vampire kung fu. As I got more confident in my abilities, I could feel my strength increasing. It's like I feel more alive (or more undead, to be accurate).

By the end of the day I'd learned the vam-pire leap, the ghoul jab, the night-stalker punch, and the undead roundhouse kick. I'm off to practice these again in the garden now.

FRIDAY, JUNE 24
2:00 p.m.

I must have looked worried this morning because Mum made a lovely warm bowl of type B+ to cheer me up. She seems more concerned than Dad at the prospect of losing me for a century. She said that all she ever wanted was to settle down to a quiet family life and didn't see why vampires like Vaclav (this is the name they use for Mr. Jenkins) couldn't just forgive and forget.

Much as I hate Mr. Jenkins, I wouldn't say his behavior was entirely unjustified. From what I can gather, Dad transformed him over two hundred years ago by accidentally infecting him with vampire blood while feeding on him. He then refused to let Mr. Jenkins join his coven and wouldn't even train him in basic vampire survival, forcing him to spend the next few decades drinking the blood of rats in the sewers of Prague.

When I asked Mum why Dad behaved like this, she said that he was a different vampire back then and would often drink too much blood and show off. She says that he's changed now.

No wonder Dad was so embarrassed when he was giving me that talk about safe feeding. It's clearly not advice he's followed! I wonder how many other disgruntled vampires are lurking around waiting to get revenge?

6:00 p.m.

Chloe popped round again after school, courageously breaking the terms of her grounding once more. I asked her if she would join me in exile if I lost, and she said she'd have to find out about the local schools first to check if she could still do business studies, English literature, and psychology for A level. At least this shows she's been thinking seriously about the possibility.

She looked upset as she said good-bye. But this is what happens when you date a dangerous supernatural being. If she wanted a mundane suburban life, she should have stuck with Wayne.

12:00 a.m.

I must say I'm somewhat concerned by all this talk about Dad transforming humans by mistake in the past. I hope I wasn't an accident!

## SATURDAY, JUNE 25

I'm feeling nervous about tonight's duel now. Part of me just wants to surrender and take my exile, but a hundred years is a long time. Imagine all the computer games I'll miss if Mr. Jenkins sends me somewhere with no electricity.

They'll be on to the PlayStation 40 by the time I'm back.

Dad has given me a leather holster with a solid gold stake in it. It feels unwieldy, but Dad says it's part of the vampire duel tradition. To make your opponent formally concede, you must pin him down and hold the stake over his heart. They used to give you genuine wooden ones, but they were outlawed by the Vampire Council's Health and Safety Division in 1881.

When I strapped on the holster, it made me realize how serious all of this is. Mr. Jenkins has had full control of his vampire powers for two hundred years, while I've only had a week to get the hang of mine. Let's just say that if the Vampire Council's Gambling Division was still going, they wouldn't be offering very good odds on me.

# SUNDAY, JUNE 26

I went down to the park with Mum and Dad an hour early to warm up for the duel. Mr. Jenkins turned up just before twelve, looking smug and confident.

I was ready to start straightaway, but it turns out that vampire duels are stuffy and formal occasions. As I stood facing Mr. Jenkins, my dad unfurled a large scroll and read out the 137 rules of vampire conflict set out by the Vampire Council in 1717. It was really boring, and I stopped concentrating after a while, so I've no idea what exactly I agreed to.

By the time the duel itself started, it was almost 1:00 a.m., and I'd lost a lot of the energy I'd been building up. Mr. Jenkins didn't waste any time, launching with a quick jab that broke my nose. Dad had taught me how to block these, but

I didn't remember in time. I backed away to give my nose a chance to mend, and Mr. Jenkins came forward with a flying kick that knocked me to the floor and cracked two of my ribs.

Although I managed to get up pretty quickly, I found it hard to summon the same ferocity of attack as last week. I think this was partly because I'd started to feel sorry for Mr. Jenkins since Mum had told me about Dad's mistreatment of him. I wish Mum had waited until after the duel to tell me there were two sides to the story.

Nonetheless, I landed a couple of solid blows on Mr. Jenkins. He retaliated with a fast kick, but I swung out of his way. I was beginning to feel my strength and speed picking up now and was able to match anything Mr. Jenkins offered, but every time I made a move, he blocked it. Instead, I retreated, and Mr. Jenkins did the same.

We both waited, and then we both charged. I tried to strike Mr. Jenkins with one of the roundhouse kicks I'd been practicing, but I misjudged the move and he pulled me down to the floor. I struggled about but couldn't get free of his grasp. He then pulled his ceremonial stake out of his backpack and ordered me to surrender.

Just as I was about to formally concede, though, I summoned my last ounce of energy, and a strange image came into my mind. I saw a leaf, then an acorn, and then the bark of a tree. I felt like I was running down a tree and then through huge blades of grass toward the silhouette of a man holding a large stake. I felt the weight lift from my body, and when my sight was clear again, Mr. Jenkins was writhing around on the floor, covered in vicious squirrels!

I got to my feet and realized that my chance had come. I put my foot on Mr. Jenkins's neck and held my stake over him. I asked him if he surrendered, and he said that I'd broken the rules by failing to declare my powers of animal mind control. I told him that I'd never done it before, so I could hardly be expected to declare it. After a few more grumbles he gave in. The squirrels scurried back up the trees.

When Mr. Jenkins asked for the terms of his exile, I didn't have the heart to go through with my equator plan. I sent him to Alaska, which has always been a popular destination with vampires, and my only condition was that he didn't look for employment as a PE teacher. I saw no reason to make future generations endure what I've had to.

Mum said that I'd showed compassion worthy

of the ancient vampire nobility and the best animal control she'd seen for decades. She hasn't been this proud of me since I passed Grade 8 Piano.

I rang Chloe to tell her that I had won, and she was overjoyed, although she had to whisper, because she isn't supposed to use her cell phone after ten.

## MONDAY, JUNE 27

I went back to school today. In assembly the principal announced that Mr. Jenkins had quit his job effective immediately due to a "family emergency." I looked at Chloe and smiled, but we couldn't say a word about what had really happened over the last few days.

I feel really good after my victory. I no longer think of myself as boring old Nigel Mullet, but

Nigel of Stockfield, master of vampire martial arts and animal mind control. And very tough to beat on Mario Kart.

## TUESDAY, JUNE 28

Sarah from the popular gang passed a note round in math today saying that she fancies me. At first I thought it was a wind-up, but when I glanced across at her, she blushed and looked away. Chloe ripped the note up when she saw it. I hope it made her realize what a catch she has!

This evening I looked at my face in the mirror to see if any vampire attractiveness had appeared. Something must have changed since the girls from the popular gang gave me four out of ten for looks, but I can't see what.

## WEDNESDAY, JUNE 29

Thanks to the exile of Mr. Jenkins, we had a substitute teacher called Mr. Moss for PE today. I didn't bother with any excuses, as I actually want to do PE now I've got my vampire speed and strength. Obviously, I'd give myself away if I used them too much, but I can still switch them on just enough to be the best in the class.

In the gym, everyone was shocked at how easily I jumped over the vaulting horse and climbed up the ropes. I even went right to the top of the climbing wall and saw the gap where I ripped out the pole in my first conflict with Mr. Jenkins. Nobody seems to have noticed it yet.

At the end of the lesson, Mr. Moss said that I should join a gymnastics club! After all the

shocks I've suffered over the past few weeks,
this has to be the biggest yet—a PE teacher
I actually like.

## THURSDAY, JUNE 30

This morning Craig stuck a pound coin to the
floor with superglue as a practical joke. He was
waiting a few feet away and jeering at anyone
who tried to pick
it up. When I
attempted
to lift

the coin, I uprooted the whole paving slab it was glued to. I must be more careful about keeping my vampire strength under wraps.

This afternoon I found out that two more girls from the popular gang like me! At first I was worried that someone might have told them I'm a vampire, but there's no way they can know. Perhaps I'm developing supernatural beauty. Or perhaps I'm just making more eye contact now. I don't know. It's all very confusing.

I remembered my vow to get revenge on the girls from the popular gang if they ever started liking me, but I couldn't really be bothered. I have no interest in their shallow little world now.

## FRIDAY, JULY 1

I had fun playing around with my animal mind-control power today. I looked at the neighbor's cat from my bedroom window and concentrated on it until I could see the world through its eyes. Cats must get so bored of looking at everything in black and white.

I made it jump up a tree, roll over on its back, and then stroke its head with its paw before I let it go. It gave me a really dirty look and then dashed away before I could control it again.

## SATURDAY, JULY 2

Chloe's grounding has finished now, so we went to the countryside to test out my powers. We found a nice deserted spot, and Chloe set me a series of challenges. First, I scaled a cliff face and jumped down again. Then I threw a huge rock across a river. My next challenge was to go through an entire forest without letting my feet touch the ground, but I fell down and broke my ankle, and we had to wait for it to heal.

When it was better, she set me a challenge to see how high in the air I could jump, but after a while I got worried that someone would see me from the road so I stopped.

## SUNDAY, JULY 3
### 7:00 a.m.

Dad has agreed to drive me to the zoo today. I have some payback planned for all the animals that tried to ruin my life on the school trip.

### 6:00 p.m.

I had fun on my trip to the zoo today, and I'd like to think I made the experience more enjoy-able for all the other visitors.

As soon as the animals saw me, they started to freak out, just as they had last time. They soon went quiet when they realized what I had in store for them, though. I stared right into the eyes of a meerkat that was standing guard on top of its enclosure. I got inside its mind and made it wobble from side to side as if it were drunk and then fall flat on its back. Everyone around the cage started filming it on their phones, so I made it do the same thing over and over again.

I left the meerkat and entered the mind of an orangutan, which I made pull some funny expressions and fall off a tire. As I stalked around the zoo, I made a baby elephant sneeze, a gorilla moonwalk, and a giraffe pull a branch with its mouth so that it flew right back in its face.

This is what you get for messing with me, animal kingdom. I condemn you to the humiliation of becoming a cute Internet clip. Now you're the ones everyone is laughing at.

## MONDAY, JULY 4

I was feeling brave today, so I came right out and asked Chloe if she was ready to let me drink her blood. She seemed quite shocked at first, but she became more open to the idea once I explained to her that if I drink just a little bit, it won't do her any harm.

Obviously, if I get greedy and drink loads, she'll be ill for a couple of days, but I didn't tell her that because I'm sure I've got the willpower to hold back.

Chloe said that she trusts me, but she doesn't feel ready just yet.

## TUESDAY, JULY 5

I asked Dad for a thousand pounds to buy Chloe a diamond pendant, but he came out with the same old tripe about us drawing attention to ourselves if we spend too much. I don't know why he can't make an exception for something as important as this.

In the end he gave me twenty pounds and I bought Chloe a bat-shaped pendant from the Goth shop. She was very pleased with it

and let me fasten it around her neck. I thought she might be so overwhelmed by my generosity that she would let me have a feed, but no such luck.

I don't mind, though. I can be patient.

## WEDNESDAY, JULY 6

We played soccer in PE today and I scored four goals. I could have scored a fifth, but I was scared of revealing my powers, so I struck it wide.

## THURSDAY, JULY 7

I'm trying to find a new hobby to occupy my mind while Chloe makes her decision. So far I've attempted gardening, juggling, and learning about dinosaurs. None of them helped me, but I will be strong.

I'm sure Chloe will agree soon, but in the meantime I'll just have to suck it up. Or, rather, not suck it up.

## FRIDAY, JULY 8

I went out for a run tonight. I only intended to go as far as the park, but I got really in the zone, and when I stopped, I was surprised to find myself at the seaside. I must be careful not to run past any speed cameras. The last thing I want is grainy footage of me dashing around at fifty miles an hour turning up on the Internet.

## SATURDAY, JULY 9

I tried to write a poem today, but I have to admit it's not up to my usual standard.

# LET US WANDER TOGETHER

Let us wander together
Through endless night
Surveying the world
By pale moonlight
Then you will let me
Sip your blood
It will be really nice
It will be really good


I'm especially disappointed by the ending, but I couldn't think of anything else. How strange that all the time I was in despair, great art was flowing from my pen, but now that I've found contentment, this is the best I can do.

I don't really care, though. If misery is the price you have to pay for genius, count me out.

Let someone else take on the responsibility of being the greatest poet of a generation.

## SUNDAY, JULY 10

Chloe came round today, and I practiced my mesmerism skills on her. It's quite tricky, but I think I'm getting the hang of it. I can now give Chloe just enough hypnosis so that she comes round again after a couple of minutes.

## MONDAY, JULY 11

Went to school today. Then went for a walk with Chloe. Then came home and had type-AB+ blood for dinner.

## TUESDAY, JULY 12

Quite sunny today. Chloe came round after school.

This is my first diary entry for a while, and I think it will also be my last.

Summer vacation starts today, and now that I've finally got my vampire powers, I'd rather be outside enjoying myself than moping around in here.

Also, Chloe says she's ready to let me drink her blood, and I don't think it would be gentlemanly of me to write down anything about that, even in a secret diary.

She told me recently that she wouldn't mind if she did turn into a vampire. She said that I'm one and I seem to be enjoying myself. And she's right, I have been enjoying myself recently, I really have.

But I still wouldn't recommend it to anyone. The first one hundred years were terrible.